Leo Kessler is a familia
In addition to his nume
the author of several no
screenplay *Breakthrough*

Also by Leo Kessler

The *SS Assault Regiment Wotan* Series
SS PANZER BATTALION
DEATH'S HEAD
CLAWS OF STEEL
GUNS AT CASSINO
THE DEVIL'S SHIELD
HAMMER OF THE GODS
FORCED MARCH
BLOOD AND ICE
THE SAND PANTHERS
COUNTER-ATTACK
PANZER HUNT
SLAUGHTER GROUND
HELLFIRE
FLASHPOINT
CAULDRON OF BLOOD
SCHIRMER'S HEADHUNTERS
WHORES OF WAR

The *Stormtroop* Series
STORMTROOP
BLOOD MOUNTAIN
VALLEY OF THE ASSASSINS
RED ASSAULT
HIMMLER'S GOLD
FIRE OVER KABUL

The *Rommel* Series
GHOST DIVISION
MASSACRE

The *Otto Stahl* Series
OTTO'S PHONEY WAR
OTTO'S BLITZKRIEG!
OTTO AND THE REDS

The *Sea Wolves* Series
SINK THE SCHARNHORST
DEATH TO THE DEUTSCHLAND

Also:

As Klaus Konrad
The *Russian Series*
FIRST BLOOD
MARCH ON MOSCOW
FRONT SWINE

Leo Kessler

Schirmer's Death Legion

Wotan 18

Futura
Macdonald & Co
London & Sydney

A Futura Book

First published in Great Britain in 1983
by Futura Publications, a Division of
Macdonald & Co (Publishers) Ltd
London & Sydney

ISBN 0 7088 2246 0

Filmset, printed and bound in Great Britain by
Hazell Watson & Viney Ltd, Aylesbury, Bucks

Futura Publications
A Division of
Macdonald & Co (Publishers) Ltd
Maxwell House
74 Worship Street
London EC2A 2EN

'When y're wounded and left . . . and the women come out to cut up what remains. Jest roll on yer rifle and blow out yer brains! And go to your Gawd like a soldier . . . Go, go, go like a soldier.'

Rudyard Kipling: *The Young British Soldier*

A MISSION IS PROPOSED

'When we rode hell-for-leather, both squadrons together,
That didn't care whether we lived or we died.'

Rudyard Kipling: *Shilling a Day*.

ONE

It was unbearably hot.

The sky over Algiers glowed like a furnace. Not a breath of wind stirred. The sea below was a deep motionless blue, the light a brilliant white. It cut the eye like the blade of a sharp knife. In the gutters the skinny-ribbed mongrels panted listlessly, too hot and weary to scavenge for the mutton and chicken bones tossed outside the bistros and cafés the previous night.

Slowly, very slowly, the little procession of mules and barefoot desert Arabs, muffled in their dirty white *jellabas*, wound their way up the steep hill towards the *kasbah*, watched by the Mozabite shopkeepers who lounged in the dark doorways of their bullet-scarred shops like fat, limp slugs.

Everywhere there was barbed wire. Heaped sandbags protected all public buildings, with iron grilles newly installed in front of the café windows to protect them from the hand-grenades the terrorists had begun to fling at their patrons, as they roared by on their little second-hand motor-cycles. At fifty-metre intervals along the steep incline there were small concrete blockhouses, guarded by pale-faced, frightened French recruits in overlarge steel helmets, sweat-damp forefingers permanently clamped around their trig-gers. This day, hate and fear were palpable in the the sun-baked streets of the African capital. Tension was in the air. Something was going to happen – and happen soon.

The little convoy stopped at the entrance to the *kasbah*. From his stork-legged watchtower guarding the entrance, the unseen French commander called out his questions, and the leader of the column, a giant of a fellow, bellowed back his answers in broken French, holding up his permit all the while, as if the Frenchman could see the photograph on it at that distance.

'*Passez, sales cons!*' the officer called finally, and the weary convoy started to enter, covered by the machine-gunners of the watchtower; for the desert Arabs were about to enter enemy territory. For months now the *kasbah* had been under the command of the rebels. In this dangerous summer of 1956 no Frenchman would dare enter that sinister world outside the law. He would not survive five whole minutes. Gradually, the *kasbah* swallowed them up and the French soldiers high above the ground relaxed again.

In single file the convoy of drivers and mules passed through the staired passages, cut like dark gulleys into the mountainside. On both sides there were dim, cave-like booths, lit by the glow of charcoal fires or by olive-oil lamps. The sultry air was heavy with the scent of garlic and cous-cous. Slowly, with the disdain of the desert Arab written all over their dark, hawk-like faces, the drivers elbowed their way through the congested passageways, filled with Jewish peddlers, coal-black Nubian servants, *hadji*, with their rich yellow or gold turbans indicating that they had made the pilgrimage to Mecca, beggars exposing their sores or lying limbless in the gutter next to their bowls.

They passed through the Street of the Coopersmiths, loud with the clanging of hammers beating out coffee pots and charcoal braziers. They fought their way through a souk, crowded with veiled peasant women who had brought their produce in to sell at the little stalls. On through the Street of the Tailors, the men and their apprentices sitting cross-legged on their low tables, stitching busily at the *serwals*, the baggy breeches favoured by country-folk. The big Arab, who seemed to be the leader, hawked and spat contemptuously into the dust at their feet, muttering something about 'filthy infidel Jews', as he passed each tailor.

Now they were almost through the *kasbah*. The exit gate was only five hundred metres away, and still the desert Arabs with their heavily laden mules did not seem to have found what had brought them here. At the entrance to the Rue Mormol, the walls decorated with the usual painted rebel slogans and the customary *instigfal* – 'liberation' – their gigantic leader held up his dark hand for them to halt.

Gratefully, the others slumped over their donkeys' backs, skinny hands holding onto the loads for support, while the giant stared around him, as if looking for something specific. To the left there was another souk, swarming with merchants and languid customers. To the right there was the brothel that went with the souk; fat, blousy, painted women leaning out of the windows, with a bored guard, ancient rifle slung carelessly over his shoulder, lounging at the door, moodily eating a tin bowl of cold white beans. Ahead of them there was perhaps the only straight length of road in the whole of the *kasbah*, leading to the exit gate.

The giant frowned. Behind him the others appeared to sleep. There was no sound save the muted chatter of the dealers in the souk. Up at the windows the waiting whores smoked silently, it was too warm for them to indulge in their usual silly chatter. A dog cocked its leg and urinated against the side of the guard eating beans. He did not seem to notice.

Abruptly, the giant did the same. He raised his right leg and loosed a long, low, satisfying and not unmusical fart. It was one known and respected in sergeants' messes, both German and French, from Oslo in the north to Oran in the south; and from St Nazaire on the western coast of France to Smolensk in the east of Russia. Suddenly the sleeping Arabs were galvanized into hectic activity. They threw off their long camel-hair robes to reveal the mottled camouflage tunics of the Foreign Legion below, grabbing for their machine-pistols the very next instant.

'*Lizards!* . . . *It's the lizards!*[1]' one of the fat whores screamed hysterically, and dropped a second later as a wild flurry of slugs stitched a lethal pattern of lead just underneath her window.

[1] Algerian nickname for the Foreign Legion soldiers on account of their camouflage uniforms.

At the door of the brothel the Arab sentry fiddled with his rifle-strap. Too late. Sergeant-Major Schulze sprang forward. He raised his steam-shovel of a fist. The brass knuckles – his beloved 'Hamburger Equalizer' – gleamed momentarily in the sun. Next moment they smashed right into the man's dark face. Bone splintered. Blood jetted from his shattered nostrils. Spitting out fragments of teeth in a crimson gore, he sank to the dust, as Schulze sprang over him, crying the battle-cry of Schirmer's Headhunters: *'Alles fuer Deutschland! . . . ALLES FUER DEUTSCHLAND!'*

Schulze's foot lashed out. The door splintered and went flying back on shattered hinges. Schulze crouched. From the hip, he let rip a burst into the dark interior, pungent with the cheap scent of the whores. The noise was ear-splitting. A hook-nosed Arab with an automatic in his hand fell, reeling blindly along the wall. Schulze rushed in, coughing in the acrid fumes.

A fat man in striped lounging pyjamas came running out of a room to the left, hands raised in surrender, his jowls quivering with fear. 'Don't shoot . . . don't shoot,' he quavered, tears streaming down his pudgy face. *'Don't shoot!'*

'Take this one!' Schulze barked to the Headhunters crowding in behind him, while others fired swift, controlled volleys at the building's upper window to keep the occupants pinned down.

'*Schnell . . . vite . . . allez . . .* slopehead!' He aimed a tremendous kick at the fat Arab's behind and sent him reeling out into the open, already loud with the roar of powerful engines. 'You . . . you . . . *follow* me!'

Two at a time, he sprang up the rickety stairs in his big rubber-soled para boots. A grenade sailed to meet him. He ducked and it whizzed over his shoulder to explode harmlessly below. Schulze fired as he ran. An Arab screamed shrilly and tumbled over the banister. He hit the dusty marble below like a sack of wet cement.

Now the men of Schirmer's Headhunter Battalion of the French Foreign Legion swarmed through the building which Army Intelligence had fingered as the Algerian FLN's[1] HQ the day before, breaking in doors, firing swift bursts into the darkened rooms and then wading over the dead and dying, to pull out the vitally needed prisoners. Mainly German and SS, these men had been brutalized by their ten years of war in three continents and were blinded by their hatred of 'Popovs', 'gooks' and 'slopeheads'. They gave and expected no quarter. If the big bluff sergeant-major hadn't been there, they would have slaughtered the lot of them, men and women, indiscriminately. Now they raced from room to room, loud with the chatter of automatics and the high hysterical screams of the terrified whores; while down below in the street, littered with the bodies of dead Arabs, the noise of racing engines grew ever closer.

Minutes later, they had some ten or so prisoners crouching on the ground below, their hands clasped over their shaven heads, faces ashen with fear, while the Headhunters holding the streets lay in the gutters, fending off the snipers who had materialized on the rooftops to repel this surprise attack in the very heart of the rebel stronghold.

Schulze noted the return fire automatically. Pushing aside a screaming whore, who was completely naked save for black stockings and high-heeled shoes, he advanced on the tall young man with the gold pince-nez who cowered in the far end of the room, hands held stiffly in the air, crying, '*Please, don't shoot . . . please don't!*'

For a moment Schulze's eyes fell on the whore's ample breasts, standing out from her lithe brown body like two over-inflated footballs, in undisguised admiration. The rebel seized his opportunity. His right hand flashed to the back of his collar. A knife gleamed. '*Deutsches schwein,*' he snarled in good German and flung it.

Schulze ducked just in time. The whore wasn't so fortunate for the knife cut deep into her right breast and she went reeling back, clutching at the blade, her fingers already flushing scarlet with bright blood.

[1] The Algerians' liberation movement of the 1950s.

Schulze let out a tremendous cry of rage. He grabbed the tall young man by the throat, slamming him against the wall with all the strength of his brutal shoulder muscles. The man's mouth dropped open with shock. Moments later Schulze had rammed the muzzle of his machine-pistol into it, crying, beyond himself with rage, as the whore died on the floor at his feet.

'Eat lead, you brown bastard! You've just gone and killed a good piece of gash . . . *I'm gonna splatter your goddam brains all over the shitting wall!*'

'Stop it, Schulze! Knock if off now,' a well-known voice cried in highly accented German. 'We need the creep . . . *DON'T SHOOT!*'

Still holding his machine-pistol pressed deep into the rebel's mouth, Schulze turned round.

It was Major Washington Lee Lincoln Lightning, nick-named 'White Lightning', Schirmer's second-in-command. Nature had played an evil trick on the American para, formerly of the US 101st Airborne Division before he had killed a superior officer in a brawl and had deserted to Schirmer's Headhunters. His face, despite the lidless eyes, was straight from an Army recruiting poster – keen and hard, with a finely chiselled nose and a lean, tough jaw – perfect save for one thing: from birth he had not had one single hair on his body. Lacking eyebrows, facial or body hair, he was completely and utterly bald. He was indeed 'White Lightning'.

'He's the brains, you big rogue,' the American snapped casually, or so it seemed, taking aim with his .45 through the open window and bringing down a sniper on the opposite roof. 'We need him, *if* he'll talk.'

'He'll talk if that arsehole with ears, Tod, gets his pinkies on him,' Schulze said, pulling out his weapon. 'That shit could make even a mummy sing.'

Schulze took his muzzle out of the rebel's mouth and the man nearly collapsed with relief. He gave the Arab a shove and sent him reeling down the stairs to join the rest. Sadly, Schulze took a last look at the dead whore. 'Great crap on the Christmas tree,' he said to no one in particular. 'With a pair of lungs like that, the poor bitch would have gone far. A feller could have wrapped them tits around his head and not known any pain for a couple of days!' Affectionately, he bent and closed her eyelids, then he was doubling down the stairs with the snipers' bullets chipping the stone walls and showering him with plaster.

He blinked in the sudden bright light. The Headhunters were thrusting their captives into the two waiting half-tracks, while their drivers gunned the engines, as if in a hurry to be off.

'Casualties, Spider Arse?' Schulze rapped.

Sergeant Hermann, known as Spider Arse because of his strange gait, the result of having his right buttock blown off by an explosive shell at Stalingrad in '42, grinned and held up one finger. 'One,' he said, 'bought a bullet in his guts. Nothing serious. But a bit lower and he wouldn't have been much more use to the ladies.' He guffawed unfeelingly and ducked as a salvo of machine-gun bullets ripped the length of the wall just above his head.

Schulze gave a sigh of relief. They had pulled it off. It had all gone much better than he and Colonel Schirmer had expected. 'Ah, what the hell,' he said. 'You lot are a bunch of honey-bums anyway. Lot of warm brothers – wouldn't know what to do with a piece of slit even if you had it on its back with its pearly gates wide open. Come on . . . *los!* Those slopeheads on the roof are getting too close for my liking!'

Schulze and White Lightning piled into the back of the half-track, the bullets howling off its armoured sides like tropical raindrops rattling onto a tin roof.

'*Roll 'em!*' the tall lean American yelled above the racket.

The drivers needed no urging now. They slammed home their gears. With a creak and a rattle, the two White half-tracks started to move forward. A great cry of rage went up from the rebels as they began to drop from the low roofs on both sides of the road, grenades hissing through the air. Here and there, bolder rebels ran into the centre of the road and tried to knock out the sweating, harassed drivers by planting a bullet through the narrow driving slit in the armour plating. It looked as if the Headhunters were heading straight for trouble.

But Colonel Erwin Schirmer, the veteran of ten years of partisan warfare, had come fully prepared for these last critical moments of the daring raid into the *kasbah*.

Standing boldly framed in the middle of the exit gate, his cap tilted to the back of his square shaven head, a broad grin on his tough bronzed face, disfigured by the livid bayonet scar zig-zagging down the left side, he yelled, 'Mortar one . . . mortar two . . . *FIRE!*'

The crouching mortar squads, dug in at either side of the gate, ducked and fired at the very same time. Twin stomach-jarring explosions. An obscene belch. Schirmer blinked. Next instant, two dark objects were hurtling high into the bright blue sky. A moment later they were lost to sight.

Howling furiously, they came zooming down again – to smack right into the roofs on both sides of the road. A burst of violet flame. Instantly, thick white blinding smoke began to pour from the bombs, as a stream of shells, fired by the frantic, sweating crews, howled into the sky to explode the whole length of the exit road.

'*Gas . . . gas . . .*' the rebels shrieked in panic, dropping their weapons in their sudden terror, clutching their skinny brown throats dramatically as the white smoke swirled higher and higher in choking clouds. '*The French are gassing us . . .*'

Schirmer grinned at Pansy Petersen, who was in charge of the mortar squads. 'Well done, Lieutenant,' he cried as the first half-track swept through the gate in a cloud of racing dust. 'Right on target!'

Pansy Petersen, formerly of the *SS Death's Head Division*, holder of the Knight's Cross with Oak Leaves for outstanding bravery, raised his lacquered fingernails to his painted lips and blew his CO a kiss.

Schirmer grinned. His Headhunters were running true to form.

TWO

Sergeant Tod, the ex-Gestapo man who was officially the Headhunters' political officer, a term that Schirmer had borrowed from the Russians, but whose real function was still that of torturer, licked his wet slack lips and stared at the prisoner.

The rebel with the bruised faced and pince-nez tried not to shudder, but he could not help himself. He did. The German was playing with a tobacco-pouch made from the tanned skin of what appeared to be a negress's breast, complete with dun-coloured nipple.

Tod appeared not to have noticed the shudder, but he had. After the years he had spent in the cellars of Number Ten *Prinz Albrecht Strasse*[1], he could *smell* a victim's fear. He did not break the silence, but continued to play with the good luck charm that he had personally carved off the corpse of one of his prisoners, because it had appealed to his sadistic, macabre sense of humour.

Outside in the *caserne*, the Headhunters celebrated their triumph, filling themselves with cheap cognac and *pinard* supplied by Colonel Mercier of the Legion. At present they were bawling out the old SS marching songs. Soon they would begin to break up the barracks and Schirmer would have to send in the fifty-franc whores to calm them down.

Tod frowned in disgust. He hated all this drinking and fornicating with women. How clean and innocent little boys, even brown Arab boys, were in comparison with those fat, raddled, berouged whores the Headhunters

[1] Gestapo HQ in Berlin.

16

preferred. Then he forgot the drinkers and the whores and concentrated on the task at hand.

'Your *nom de guerre* is Heinrich,' he said without referring to the notes that Colonel Mercier had passed him one hour earlier. 'Your real name is Amar, and you are the son of Caïd Abd el Kader ben Mahmoudi. During the German occupation you went to Berlin and studied there until – er – our Führer died at the head of his soldiers in the last heroic struggle for the capital.'

The prisoner's swollen mouth dropped open stupidly.

'Hence, the code-name Heinrich,' Tod went on. 'Not very original, is it?'

'You've got it all very wrong,' the prisoner stuttered in excellent French. 'I am the son of a poor shopkeeper. I have never been out of the city of Algiers in all my li . . .' His protest ended in a yelp of pain as one of the two massive Headhunters flanking him brought his boot down hard on the prisoner's bare foot.

'*Deutsches Schwein*, I believe you called one of our NCOs,' Tod continued as if nothing had happened. 'Excellent German if I may say so.' Suddenly the deceptive soft tone vanished from his voice to be replaced by one of naked menace. 'Now listen, pig, I am going to ask you some questions and I want answers . . . and I want them fast!'

Almost unconsciously the prisoner tightened his bruised lips, as if already willing himself not to talk.

Behind his glasses, Tod's dark eyes gleamed with a near-sexual excitement. The prisoner was going to play games and he always enjoyed playing games with prisoners; it was even better than nice little boys. He pointed to the Army enamel pail and broom-handle that were the room's sole decoration. 'You see those,' he said, adding in a quick rasp, '*make* him see them, Corporal!'

The bigger of the two Headhunters grabbed the prisoner's curly hair and forced his head round. 'I see . . . I see,' he gasped through clenched teeth, his eyes filled with tears. '*I see!*'

'*Bon*,' Tod said. 'Well, to you, they must appear just an

ordinary bucket and a broom-handle. But they are more, you know . . . much more. Some people in my profession go in for elaborate equipment, electrodes to fasten to the genitals, special catheters to insert into the rectum, dental drilling machines . . .' He reeled off the various sadistic devices they had once used in those dark cellars below Number Ten, relishing the look on the prisoner's ashen face. 'But me,' he concluded with mock humility,' I am a simple man. I prefer those two humble objects over there. With them, as has often been said jokingly, I can make even a mummy talk.'

The prisoner made a last desperate attempt to retain his dignity. 'You will get nothing from me, German,' he said, his voice threatening to break at any moment. 'Besides, I truly know nothing . . . Nothing.'

Tod smiled benignly. 'Then we will see, won't we . . . *Corporal, put the pail on his head . . .*'

'*Merdre alors!*' Colonel Mercier, the Legion's one-armed political adviser and secret strong-man in Algeria, cursed and wiped the sweat off his cunning face, 'I have known some drinking men in my time, Schirmer, but *never* any like your Headhunters. Look at that, I beg you.' He raised himself from the cane chair and pointed over the balcony at the completely naked Headhunter down below, sprawled full-length in a horse-trough filled with dark-red *pinard*, greedily guzzling the strong wine, while other Headhunters holding small kegs of the stuff in readiness, cheered him on.

Schirmer took an amused sip of his imported whisky and smiled. 'The common soldiery, you know, my dear Mercier, they tend to entertain themselves in a rather coarse manner when they are off duty. Perhaps there is a good reason for it,' he added, with a sideways look at the Frenchman who, in 1945, had blackmailed him into joining the Foreign Legion and forming his battalion of renegade

SS men.[1] 'They probably know they are not long for this world.'

Mercier sat back and grinned. '*Touché, mon cher Schirmer . . . touché*,' he conceded. 'But this time, I do not think that they will have to sacrifice their lives unnecessarily. Algeria is not going to be another Indo-China, I promise you that.' He ran his one hand over his grizzled, cropped head. 'This time we will win.'

Erwin Schirmer made no comment. Down below, a Headhunter was running around the darkening barrack square, completely naked save for his boots and what appeared to be a fish-tail sticking out of his buttocks, crying, 'Get me, men . . . *I'm a mermaid* . . .' Crude and brutal they might be, he told himself, as another Headhunter chased after the 'mermaid' waving a mosquito curtain as if it were a fishing net, but they were his men, his children, and the Battalion was the only home he knew – *now*.

'Of course,' Mercier said with a Gallic shrug, 'the rebellion is spreading. In Paris the government is weak. As usual we are ruled by a bunch of pederasts and moneybags. But for once our military leaders are energetic and resolute. They know France and the French Army cannot stand a second Indo-China.'

'*Ah, la gloire . . . la gloire française*,' Schirmer sneered, puffing out his cheeks like French officers did when they mentioned France's glory.

Mercier was not offended. He knew Schirmer, 'your tame Boche', as his French comrades often mockingly called him. After what the tall, scarred German had been through, it was not surprising that he had become a cynic. 'You may mock, my dear fellow,' he said mildly, 'but we are not merely concerned with the fate of France this time . . . we are concerned with the fate of your own country, Germany, indeed that of the whole of Western Europe. Even the damned Americans have finally woken up to that. The rebel leaders stir up the masses with the

[1] See Kessler: *Schirmer's Headhunters* for further details.

concept of independence, but their true intention is to turn Algeria into a communist state. Once Algeria goes that way, the rest of French North Africa will follow, and British North Africa, too. From Africa it will spread to Italy and from Italy to France . . . It is like the scourge of the Middle Ages – syphilis, spread by soldiers from one country to another. No, my dear Colonel Schirmer, you and your roughnecks are not just fighting for France out here, but for Germany . . . Your homeland.'

Schirmer took another sip of his black market whisky. 'My homeland,' he whispered, almost as if speaking to himself, 'where the new people, those eager democrats in Bonn, would put me behind Swedish curtains[1] as soon as I crossed the frontier.' He laughed cynically. 'Oh yes, I'd dearly love to fight for my *homeland* out here.'

Mercier ignored the comment; perhaps he had not even heard it. 'As I said, Schirmer, we have a very good chance of winning out here this time. That rabble of clerks and shopkeepers down there in Algiers will fold soon enough, once we really tackle them. And that will be as soon as our strength here is built up. The *fellagha*[2] are tougher, a hardy country people, but without leaders and modern weapons smuggled in by the city people, they will be pretty hopeless, too. No, Schirmer, here and in the immediate countryside around the capital, we can cope with and eventually destroy the revolt, but . . .' he hesitated.

From inside the administration block came the muffled cries of pain and the steady sound of someone being struck at regular intervals. Schirmer frowned. He knew the need for torture; it was the one reliable way of obtaining information. Nevertheless he did not like it one bit, even after all the years he and his Headhunters had employed it as a routine method. '*But*,' he prompted.

'But if the revolt spreads to the Sahara Desert, then we are in real trouble.'

'To the desert tribes?'

[1] Slang for 'prison bars'.
[2] The Algerian peasantry.

'Yes. The desert stretches for thousands of kilometres, much of it uncharted, even now, thirty odd years since our first expedition crossed it in 1922. If the desert tribes joined the rebels, our resources would be stretched to the utmost limit. We'd have to pull the troops out of the coastal cities to guard the supply dumps, the road network of the Littoral, the outlying farms, the Legion's desert forts,' he shrugged a little helplessly. 'It would be the El Krim business all over[1] again, complicated by the fact that he would be supported by the city folk, their money, and,' he emphasized the words grimly, '*Russian weapons!*'

'Are you sure?'

'I'm not certain, Schirmer, but it's on the cards. The Russians are moving into North Africa. Soon they'll start popping up all over the place – Libya, Egypt, Morocco, Algeria – you'll see. They'll have their dirty red fingers in every pie, just as they had back in Indo-China.'

Schirmer nodded his understanding. Over at the barracks, his drunken Headhunters were now playing parachutists without parachutes, dropping from the upper windows to the straw mattresses spread out below. Soon, he told himself, they'd be too drunk to hit the mattresses. In the morning the Battalion's bone-menders would have the usual broken legs and arms to attend to. Still, cost what it may in damaged bodies, his Headhunters had the right to let off steam any way they wanted. Most of them wouldn't survive the year anyway. He cupped his big, scarred hands to his mouth and cried, 'Come on, let's see some real fancy jumps! You don't want to live for ever, do you, you dogs!'

Next moment Sergeant-Major Schulze came flying out of a third floor window in a shower of broken glass. He was naked save for his helmet, with a red rose tucked behind his right ear, and a jock strap. 'Get me,' he yelled, 'I'm a frigging fairy!'

Schirmer winced.

'So you see, Schirmer,' Mercier continued as Schulze

[1] Famous rebel of the twenties.

hit the pile of mattresses with a great whack, 'the import-
ance of the Caid's son, the man your fellow is working on
in there. He knows Europe, he is a known Marxist, and he
is the son of the most influential of the desert Caids, old
Abd el Kader ben Mahmoudi. The old fellow must be well
into his dotage now – after all, he was in his fifties when he
fought at the side of El Krim – and he is a devout Muslim.
But still, such old warriors never worry about the political
background to a struggle. For them all that counts is the
excitement, the passion, the glory of conflict.'

Mercier's cunning eyes gleamed enthusiastically and
Schirmer grinned. The old war horse dearly missed battle,
but with his one flipper he would be helpless in action, he
knew it. 'I shit on the *excitement*, the *passion*, the *glory* of
conflict, Mercier!' he said crudely. 'All I want to know is
what role my Headhunters are to play in this affair?'

'This, Schirmer. Your men are wasted in the cities. They
are the best anti-partisan fighters in the whole of the
French Army. They need to be out in the mountains and
the deserts stopping the desert tribes before it . . '

'. . . It's too late.' Schirmer beat him to it.

'Exactly, Schirmer.'

'But where do we start, Mercier?' Schirmer asked a little
helplessly, as the muffled moans from inside the Admin
Block assailed his ears again. 'You have said yourself that
the desert is very big and mostly uncharted. How do we
deal with these desert tribes if they are scattered everywhere?'

By way of an answer, Mercier jerked his thumb behind
him. 'I am hoping, Schirmer, that your little perverted
thug in there will give us the answer to that particular
question.' He reached for the bottle. 'Another glass of this
excellent black market firewater, *mon ami*?'

Schirmer frowned but held out his glass all the same,
Suddenly he shivered, in spite of the sticky evening heat.
Instinct warned him there was trouble ahead for Schirmer's
Headhunters. Bad trouble . . .

THREE

'*Sale cochon, leve toi!*' Tod wiped the thick opaque beads of sweat from his narrow forehead and bellowed his command down at the figure slumped in a pool of his own urine on the floor. The stench of faeces was overpowering. Tod nodded to one of the guards, both of whom were now stripped to the waist in the night heat, their brawny chests glistening with perspiration.

The Headhunter gave the prisoner a routine kick in the ribs and, as the Algerian groaned, lifted the pail off his head. The man's face was in a terrible state. A solid hour of pounding the pail with the broom-handle had turned it into a mass of purple jellied bruises. Both eyes were puffed and closed to narrow slits, and black congealed blood hung from his nostrils and ear lobes. Most of his front teeth had been shattered.

Without Tod having to give an order, the other guard marched over to the corner, ripped open his flies, let loose a stream of dark yellow urine into an empty ration can – to return and fling it straight into the semi-conscious man's face.

The prisoner gasped with shock and his eyes flicked open painfully. 'What . . .'

He did not complete the question, for Tod bent down, a look of distaste on his cruel face and, inserting both his fingers into the prisoner's broken nose, ripped the nostrils up hard. Dark red blood streamed anew down his mouth. The Algerian gagged as if about to choke, as blood and urine trickled from his chin to the floor.

Tod looked down at him contemptuously, his legs spread

apart, hands poised on his hips, calculatingly posed in such a manner. It was his favourite stance and one which gave him tremendous pleasure. It made him feel like a conqueror.

'So, you think you won't talk, eh? Well let me tell you this, pig. That was just the softening up process – just an ordinary, minor work-out.' He held up the broom-handle. 'But my poor unfortunate friend, the pole, can be put to so many uses.' He ran his tongue along his slack, drooling bottom lip, as if in anticipation. 'Just imagine what it would do to your internal plumbing if I inserted this object into your rectum for – say – no more than thirty minutes. With a little brute force – and my comrades here have the necessary muscle – I think we could ruin your sphincter for good. And do you know what that would mean? No? Then I shall tell you. You would not be able to control your waste products any more. For the rest of your life, you'd have to run around with a little plastic bag attached to your rectum.'

'A proper shitbag, you might say,' the larger of the two Headhunters added with a coarse guffaw.

'Exactly, Meier,' Tod agreed. 'A shitbag in all senses of that rather crude expression.'

Outside, the barracks had settled down. Half an hour earlier the CO had brought in the whores, so now the square was empty save for a drunken Sergeant-Major Schulze bawling – in between scooping up huge draughts of *pinard* out of the trough with his helmet – '*The captain's name was Marter . . . He was a champion farter. He could play everything . . . from God save the King . . . to Beethoven's Fourth Sonata . . .*'

Tod frowned angrily. The drunken ditty was spoiling the dignity of the occasion. Hastily he shut his mind to it, concentrating on his task with all the energy of the veteran professional that he was. 'Then again, prisoner, I could use the broom-handle on your genitals for – say – fifteen to thirty minutes. I should imagine after that, you would be of no use to those filthy whores that your kind frequent . . .

In short, pig, you are now going to speak, or leave this room crippled for life.'

He let the words sink in while the prisoner swayed back and forth as if he were drunk, giving off strange whistling sounds between his bruised swollen lips, thin jets of scarlet blood erupting from inside his shattered mouth every time he did so.

'Now, pig, I shall ask you three simple questions. You will give me three simple answers.' He nodded to Meier, and the latter jerked up the prisoner's greasy black head so that he was looking up at his tormentor through his puffed-up slits of eyes, his face contorted with agony.

'Here they are.' Tod snapped the broom-handle against the blood-soaked floor. 'One, where is your father the Caid now?' He paused and struck the floor again, 'Two, why were you in Algiers? . . . Three,' he hit the tiles a third time, 'how are the communist arms being smuggled into the country?' He raised his voice to an impressive bellow. 'Now, pig, *speak or suffer!*'

With the last of his strength, knowing instinctively that his action would result in his death, sooner or later, the tortured man hawked. Next moment he spat directly into Tod's cruel yellow face.

The ex-Gestapo man sprang back, pale with shock. Prisoners were not supposed to retaliate. With the Algerian's spittle dripping down his left cheek, he screamed, high and hysterical like a woman: '*Meier . . . Dirkmann, attend to the filthy swine!*'

A flood of icy water hit the Algerian full in the face. He gasped with shock and came to, spluttering and gasping for air. He blinked several times. His vision was blurred and somehow he could not seem to open his eyes properly. Above him, a bright white light burnt down mercilessly. Somewhere there was a strange rushing sound. What in Allah's name was it?

Brown para boots with thick rubber soles entered the far

edge of his area of vision. One drew back. He watched, seeing it like a blurred, flickering early movie. Next moment the boot thudded into his rib cage. He screamed with pain. As the broken rib plunged deeper into his lung, fresh blood started to pour from his gaping mouth once again. The strange rushing sound continued. The air was becoming appreciably colder.

'I have played with you long enough,' Tod said from far, far away. 'With pigs like you, it does not pay to be humanitarian or attempt to appeal to reason. So, you must learn the hard way.' The boots moved away again and the tormented man closed his eyes gratefully, though the sound still disturbed him – he did not know why.

'*Fertig*,' Meier called. '*Die Wanne ist jetzt voll.*'

'*Bone . . . also los!*'

Suddenly the Algerian felt his feet being seized. Cruelly, he was dragged across the cold tiles. He opened his eyes. He was in a large bathroom, whose walls, instead of being the normal bright white, were stained dark red with blood. 'What . . . what,' he began, but he did not succeed in completing the sentence.

A large hand grabbed him by the scruff of the neck and cut off his anxious question. Another grabbed his feet. The Algerian found himself being lifted easily, as if he did not weigh more than a baby. He stared down. Below him there was a big army bath filled to the brim with cold water.

Abruptly, with a surge of naked terror, he realized what they were going to do to him. Desperately, he attempted to kick out. The man holding his feet held on easily. Next moment he felt his head being forced under the water. He opened his mouth instinctively and it was flooded with water. Frantically, he fought for breath as the water swept down and filled his lungs. He struggled and squirmed like a madman, but there was no escaping that vice-like grip.

A great roaring blackness threatened to engulf him. His lungs were about to burst. Silently but hysterically he screamed for mercy. Red and silver stars exploded in front of his eyes. A minute longer and he was going to die. He couldn't hold on . . .

Suddenly he found himself face-down on the wet tiles, sobbing fervently for air, retching miserably, blood-tinged water soaking out of his gaping mouth like that of a hooked, stranded fish.

Tod waited a moment and then he snapped, 'All right, pig, where is your father, the Caid?' The para boot thudded into his broken ribs to emphasize the question and he yelped with pain, a pain which shot through his tortured body with electric intensity.

The pain did the trick. It cleared his head for a few moments and he saw that he was fighting for his life – and the cause. He had taken the beatings with the stick, but he could not stand the bath torture for long. He would either talk or drown miserably in the tub. What was he to do?

'*Fight for time!*' an urgent voice hissed at the back of his skull. '*Tell them some things, but not all . . . Play for time, in Allah's name . . . and then . . .*'

He did not think that thought to an end. Instead he heard himself saying, 'My father . . . El Caid . . . he's in the desert . . . with the . . . tribes.'

Tod's beady dark eyes gleamed behind his steel-rimmed schoolmaster's spectacles. 'Ah, ah, my friend, now you are learning sense at last. Didn't I tell you I could make anyone talk – even the bravest of men – in the end. *Bon . . . bon.* Now then, what is the link between the city FLN and the tribesmen?'

'A cigarette, please. In God's name, give me a cigarette, I will tell all!' the Algerian pleaded, hands raised in the classical pose of supplication, 'I must steady my nerves.'

Tod relented. He nodded at Meier.

The big Headhunter with the broken nose fished in his pocket and brought out of a crumpled packet of Gauloise. Without saying a word, Meier thrust one into the prisoner's swollen mouth, and when he saw that the Algerian's hands trembled too much for him to hold the match, he lit the cigarette for him.

Keeping his eyes lowered so that they could not see the look of new determination in them, the prisoner puffed greedily at the last cigarette he would smoke on this earth, while the Germans talked among themselves in bored tones and Tod waited.

The barracks were absolutely silent now, save for the steady tread of the sentries on the gravel walks outside the Legion fort. The night cloaked the barracks and its dread secrets in a thick warm darkness.

'All right,' Tod snapped suddenly. He was impatient to get on and hurry over to wake Mercier and Schirmer with the secrets he had discovered this night. 'Take the cigarette out of his mouth, Meier.'

Obligingly, the Headhunter with the broken nose did as he was ordered and the Algerian savoured his final taste of scented tobacco. Once again he faced up to his terrible ordeal and the crucial decision he was forcing himself to take, although his whole being shrieked out against what he knew he must do – soon.

Tod leaned forward. 'Now then, why are you in Algiers? What is the son of one of the most important tribal leaders doing associating with the riff-raff of the *kasbah*, meeting them in a third-rate knocking shop, eh?'

Out of the corner of his eye, the prisoner now became aware of the tall window which reached from ceiling to floor. It was of the kind popular in the twenties, with idealized figures of tall, very white soldiers in the kepis of the Legion receiving homage from kneeling peasants in turbans. The glass looked very thin and he knew the bathroom was located some three storeys up above the barracks square.

'Did you hear my question?' Tod rasped, brutally cutting into his fearful reverie. 'Why were you here?'

He bit his lip. He couldn't do it – *yet* – though he knew he must. Let Allah grant him another few moments of precious life. Why must he die so young without ever seeing the achievement of the blessed cause they had all worked so long for? 'To arrange a meeting,' he whispered, his gaze fixed on the wet floor.

'What kind of meeting?' Tod asked eagerly, knowing that he was really on to something. There would be a reward for this one. Colonel Mercier was always very generous with his secret funds on such occasions; there'd be money enough for boys, several of them, if he wished.

'Between the members of the town FLN and the tribal leaders,' he answered, his voice so low that the other three had to strain hard to catch his words.

'Where?'

He bit his bottom lip till the blood started to flow again. He couldn't answer *that* question.

Tod didn't hesitate; the prisoner must not be allowed to stall now. '*In die Wanne mit ihm,*' he commanded.

The two Headhunters grabbed the Algerian and tossed him into the bath. Water swamped everywhere as he struck his head on the side of the tub and instantly the liquid flushed red. Meier grabbed his victim's ankles and tugged. He went under. Scarlet stars exploded before his eyes. Bubbles of escaping air shot to the surface. His lungs seemed about to burst. Crazily he writhed back and forth, trying to break the terrible hold they had on him. He urinated with fear. Next moment he defecated. Now he knew he was drowning. It could only be a matter of seconds. A dull roar filled his ears. He was going . . . going . . .

Suddenly he was upright again, gasping for air. Red vomit streaming down the front of his robe. 'I'll talk . . . talking now,' he panted frantically. 'Not that . . . please, not that!'

'Then where?' Tod rasped, while Meier and the other Headhunter leaned forward like rapacious wolves.

'The Red Oasis . . .'

'Where –'

Tod was caught completely off guard. One moment the prisoner was sitting at the edge of the bath, fighting with the last of his strength for air, the next, he had pushed Tod to one side so that he blundered into Meier. Meier stumbled against the wall. The prisoner did not wait for a second invitation. He dodged the foot thrust out by the second Headhunter to stop him and ran, staggering crazily like a drunk, for the floor-to-ceiling window.

'*Halt!*' Tod cried desperately, sensing instinctively what their prisoner was going to do. '*I order you to halt, pig!*' Frantically he fumbled with his pistol holster while Meier recovered himself and bolted after the man, thus preventing Tod from firing.

The Algerian drew on his last reserves of strength. He sucked in a deep breath. The broken ribs stabbed his side like the blade of a sharp knife. With one last effort, he dived forward.

He hit the thin, coloured glass head first and it splintered instantly. The high-pitched scream of agony was ripped from his mouth by the sudden wind. He was falling, falling, falling. The cobbles of the square were coming to meet him at a tremendous rate. Seconds later, he struck the ground three storeys below at a hundred kilometres an hour. The cobbles slapped him in the face. his spine snapped. Like a rubber ball, he rose high in the air and then slammed down again, breaking every bone in his body. Once, twice, he twitched convulsively in his death agonies; then he was still, staring unseeingly at the dark velvet of the star-studded African sky.

Tod turned reluctantly while below him the barrack-room lights started to flash on and drunken male and female voices began to call out startled questions in half a dozen languages. There would be no little brown boys in this one for him . . .

FOUR

The shrill, urgent note of the bugle echoed and re-echoed throughout the snoring barracks. '*Alert . . . alert!*' harsh official voices called from below. '*Turn out the guard . . . at the double now . . . out the guard . . . !*'

Flinging aside the snoring whores who filled the entire barracks, the naked Headhunters grabbed their weapons and green-camouflage para helmets and stampeded for the square. The guard had already turned out and were staring, pertrified, at what lay just outside the barracks gate.

Schirmer, naked to the waist, automatic clasped in his big hand, skidded to a stop next to him, the angry query dying on his lips as he, too, saw what hung there on the telegraph posts.

'Holy straw sack!' Sergeant-Major Schulze gasped in horror, 'what a shitting mess!'

Just behind him one of the younger Headhunters started to vomit noisily.

Mercier clutched Schirmer's arm. '*Doucement*, Schirmer, *doucement!*' he hissed urgently, knowing just how much the big German colonel loved his rogues, almost as if they were his own children. 'It is the way that the Arab mind works, *mon ami*. They are a devious, cruel people. Last night you killed one of theirs, or so they think. This is their form of revenge.'

'But . . . but . . . *this!*' Schirmer stuttered helplessly, extending the hand still holding the automatic towards the three bodies nailed to the telegraph posts. One was set higher than the other two, but all three had their throats cut, a gory mess where their genitals had been, and what looked like a dark sausage inserted into their mouths. 'What kind . . .' He stopped, unable to find words to express his horror and bewilderment.

Mercier did not speak at once. Instead he turned to Schulze and nodded. The big red-faced NCO gestured his understanding. Wordlessly, he took a sharp bayonet from one of the ashen-faced sentries of the guard. Slowly and with dignity, almost as if this was a military ceremony, he marched forward into the ascending sun, which hung over the baked African horizon like a blood-red ball. Without a moment's hesitation he commenced sawing through the bonds of the nearest man, trying to keep his gaze averted from that terrible mutilation at the pit of his naked white stomach.

'Christ on the Cross with the two thieves,' Mercier said finally. 'Many of them are Muslim fundamentalists. It is the way that their kind would take their revenge.'

'*Revenge!*' Schirmer exploded, his eyes blazing abruptly with almost maniacal fury. 'I'll show the murdering pigs what revenge really means. They'll see how the SS deals with such matters. An eye for an eye! God in heaven, I'll show them!' Thrusting aside Mercier's restraining arm, he swung round and spotted Petersen, the homosexual, still attired in a bright floral dressing gown, his long hair neatly encased in a silken hair-net. 'You, Petersen,' he rasped harshly, 'get that damn fool gear off at once! Take out your company. Bring in bodies. At the double!'

'*Razzia?*' Petersen queried, knowing that this particular dawn there would be no tricks.

'*Razzia* . . . Bring 'em all in, men, women, children, too . . . I'll show the heathen, murdering pigs just how terrible the revenge of the SS can be . . .'

Colonel Schirmer had calmed down somewhat. Showered and shaved, he stood next to the big map of Algeria with the fan whirring softly above his square-cropped head, can of beer in one hand, listening to Colonel Mercier's analysis

of the new information obtained from the son of Caid Abd
el Kader ben Mahmoudi. By his side, an anxious White
Lightning, immaculate as ever, kept throwing worried
glances out of the open window of the office at the gate.

'From the information that Tod obtained from the fellow
before his unfortunate – er demise,' Mercier lectured, 'we
know several things. One, he was the all important link-
man between his father and the city FLN. He knew the
mentality of the desert tribesmen, of course, because he
was brought up with them. But, at the same time, he could
relate to the clerks and teachers of the city FLN, those
pseudo-intellectuals, the parlour pinks,' Mercier's red face
contorted contemptuously, 'that you always find at the
fringes of such – er – revolutionary movements, before the
real hard men take over. After all, he had been training to
be a doctor at Berlin University. He was a pseudo-intellec-
tual, too.'

Schirmer forgot his anger for a moment, trying not to
hear the scrape of shovels on the hard, stony earth behind
the fort where they were already digging the graves for his
mutilated men. 'I suppose so. Do you think that was why
he was code-named so curiously?'

'You mean his *nom de guerre* – Heinrich?' Mercier asked.
'Yes.'

Mercier frowned. 'I don't quite know. It is a funny code-
name to give to anyone out here in Africa. After all, he was
repatriated from Germany almost immediately in 1945.
Why give him a German name ten years later? Hm, let us
pass on, Schirmer. So we know that an attempt has been
made to link up the city and desert, to spread the rebellion
throughout Algeria. *Bon*, so we accept it. It is a *fait
accompli*. And we can assume that now his son is dead, the
Caid will be even more prepared to throw in his lot with
the FLN. Therefore our strategy must change. We must
strike *before* they strike!' Mercier barked.

In spite of his mood, Schirmer grinned. 'Won't that
make us war criminals, Mercier?' he queried. 'I think that

at the Nuremberg Trial back in '46[1] most of our leaders
were sentenced to death for doing exactly that.'

Mercier returned his grin, in no way put out. 'Naturally
you are right, my dear Schirmer, save for one thing.'

'What?'

Delightedly, Mercier wagged his forefinger under
Schirmer's nose. 'You *lost* the war, we won't . . . Now let us
continue. Just before the young person decided with the
exuberance of youth that he'd take a little walk out of that
third floor window, your man got the name 'Red Oasis' out
of him. Apparently that was the place where his father Caid
Abd el Kader had arranged to meet the other tribes, or at
least their leaders, in the next weeks.' He paused and looked
up at the big German colonel with his cunning, bloodshot
grey eyes significantly. 'What an opportunity that could be
for a pre-emptive strike!' he hissed suddenly.

Schirmer's eyes lit up, too. 'By God, Mercier, you are
right!' he said enthusiastically, 'we could wipe out the
whole damn bunch of them once and for all. Perhaps even
the leaders of the city FLN, too!'

'Exactly.' Mercier thrust out his one hand, fingers
extended, and then squeezed them together slowly, the
knuckles whitening with the pressure. 'Crush them once
and for all.'

White Lightning took his gaze off the gate momentarily
and said, 'But where is this – er – Red Oasis? I've been in
Algeria six months now and not heard of it.'

Mercier puffed out his cheeks in that Gallic gesture of
exasperation and said, 'My dear Major, you are the only
American I *think* I like, but if you continue to ask awkward
questions like that, I am afraid I shall begin to go off you,
too.'

Schirmer's grin vanished. 'But he's right, Mercier. I,
too, have made an intensive study of the maps of Algeria
since we were posted here from Indo-China, and I have
never heard of the place.'

Slowly and thoughtfully, Mercier walked over to the

[1] The War Trials of the German Nazi leaders.

map, his highly polished riding boots creaking as he did so. Dandy that he was, the Frenchman still affected the pre-war uniform of a Legion officer, complete with long white silk scarf and kepi tilted at the usual rakish, devil-may-care angle. He tapped the big map with his riding crop. 'As you know, Algeria is settled mainly along the fertile coastal region – the green on the map. As you progress inland, the settled regions give way to plantations and large olive farms, mostly run by our own people. After that comes the less fertile land, with Legion forts dotted all over the place to protect the coastal area from raiding Arabs. Finally we have the desert itself, perhaps some three-quarters of the country, stretching right down to Central Africa, but inhabited and dotted with an oasis here and there. Without water the desert folk cannot survive.'

'I know, Mercier,' Schirmer said impatiently. 'I don't need a lesson in elementary geography. But where is this damned *Red* Oasis?'

Mercier's eyes twinkled suddenly. 'Have you heard of the problem of Hannibal's elephants?' he asked.

Schirmer looked down at the Frenchman as if he had suddenly gone mad. '*Hannibal's elephants* . . . what in three devils' names have they got to do with it?'

'A lot, I shouldn't wonder,' Mercier answered quite calmly. 'I am sure a student of military history like yourself knows how Hannibal marched from Africa and crossed the Alps with his elephants in his campaign against the Romans.'

Schirmer nodded hurriedly.

'Well, the big question is – where did the elephants come from?'

White Lightning groaned. All this was typical of Colonel Mercier and the French in general. They loved the oblique approach. They could never say and do anything straight.

'There are no elephants here in Algeria, nor naturally in the Sahara Desert itself. But Hannibal himself was an African – from this very area. So, once again, how did he obtain his war-winning elephants?'

Schirmer did not answer. Now he could hear the slow

groan of truck engines labouring their way up the steep incline to the barracks. It would be Petersen returning with his victims.

'Some say they came from the Valley of the Guit and support this view with the evidence of the Roman general, Suetonius Paulinus. He wrote in the first century that there were elephants in the Forest of Guir, which is close to the Algerian-Moroccan frontier. I don't believe it. The only place that he could have got those elephants was in the Congo to the south, and in order to bring his – er – primitive tanks, which so scared the Romans when they came trundling out of the snows of the Alps through the backdoor into Italy . . .'

'Was through the Sahara.' White Lightning cut him short, very nervous now at the prospect of what was to come when Petersen returned from the *Razzia*, 'And that brings us to the question of the Red Oasis, because elephants need water – a helluva lot of it!'

Mercier smiled thinly, but his grey eyes did not light up. 'Ah the brashness of the New World,' he mused. 'What energy, what directness!' He shook his head in mock sadness. 'How shabby, slow, and devious we Europeans must seem in contrast. Oh yes, you are right, Major. If the elephants did cross the Sahara, they would have needed water, and since 1950 some of our scientists from the Centre of Saharan Research have been making a preliminary plot of where those oases might have been – might well still *be!*' he emphasized the word. 'If you would care to look at the map, gentlemen. Here below Colomb Bechar, our major military headquarters in the Zone of the Sahara, is the biggest Legion fort at the fringe of the desert, Beni Abbes. Now here is the last great oasis under our control, the Scorpion Oasis, to which the camel caravans come when they arrive from the Great Western Sand Desert. At this spot our people have found definite traces of a pre-Roman civilization, one that Hannibal could well have known. You understand what that means?'

Schirmer took a sip of his ice-cold beer. 'The route taken

by the Arab caravans might well be the same one taken by Hannibal.'

'*Mais oui*, and according to our people, deep in the desert there is an area spreading over several thousand kilometres – of sandstone.'

'Red sandstone?' White Lightning asked quickly, as the noise of the engines got ever closer.

'Yes, red sandstone.'

'So the Red Oasis could be located somewhere in that area,' Schirmer concluded.

'We think so,' Mercier said softly, as the first truck filled with the victims of the *Razzia* swung round the corner into the entrance of the Fort. He bit his bottom lip and suddenly visualized the national monument in Southern France at Oradour. Something like what was going to happen next had happened there too, back in 1944, when the *Waffen SS* had been irritated beyond measure by the French partisans – 'patriots', they had called themselves then – of the region and had run amok.[1] 'We think too,' he went on hurriedly, dismissing that uneasy thought, 'that if anyone can find that lost oasis on the old trading route it will be Colonel Schirmer and his Headhunters.' He forced a smile.

'But the FLN are no fools,' Schirmer objected hastily, as Schulze jumped from the first truck and slapped the canvas with a hoarse, 'Everyone out . . . come on now, *allez*, everyone out! . . . *Los, los, los dalli-dalli!*'

Mercier frowned at that '*Los, los, los*'. How many French deportees heading for the camps must have been urged on their way to the ovens by that same harsh phrase. 'What do you mean, Schirmer?'

'I mean, if we leave Algiers, they'll put two and two together. They'll know we've just killed the Caid's son after squeezing him and reason – correctly – that we're out looking for the meeting place of the tribes and their own FLN leaders, the Red Oasis. They could change their plans completely.'

[1] The village was burned to the ground and its inhabitants slaughtered in the summer of 1944.

'Agreed,' Mercier said. 'But what you intend to do next,' he indicated the frightened civilians collected in the dawn raid being huddled into the centre of the barracks square, 'will ensure that you and your men are disgraced, Schirmer – and at HQ we will certainly make sure that everyone is aware of your disgrace. You will be sent out to Beni Abbes Fort as a punishment. It is, after all, the worst assignment in the whole of the Legion. Don't we have our prison camp for murderers, deserters and scum of that kind there?'

Schirmer grinned. 'We are the Boche still, aren't we – the murderers of the SS?'

'Naturally, Schirmer, it is the sort of thing that one expects from your kind – *atrocities!*'

White Lightning gulped as the Headhunters roughly pushed their victims into line: an old woman who looked puzzled, several younger ones sobbing hysterically, a gang of youths ashen-faced and trembling, eyes following every movement made by the 'Lizards', an old man tall, erect, looking as if he might once have served in the Army of France, face full of scorn. 'Sir, must we go ahead with this?' he asked, a note of pleading in his voice.

Schirmer nodded and, dropping the can of beer, picked up his camouflage. He looked at Mercier. 'Do you wish to be present, Colonel?'

'No,' Mercier snapped, 'for obvious reasons.'

'For obvious reasons,' Schirmer echoed. 'Let the Boche do France's dirty work, eh?' He touched his hand to his cap and went out, leaving the American and the Frenchman to watch.

Schirmer looked around as they set up the machine-guns, as if it were important to imprint this place and this time on his mind's eye. It was a landscape meant for dying in, he told himself, the ground harsh, barren, sun-baked, the sky a bronzed red, like a copper coin glimpsed at the bottom of a scum-covered pool. He turned his attention to the prisoners. There was no dignity about them. They wailed, they cursed, they pleaded, falling onto the ground and wringing their skinny brown hands in abject fear and desperation – all save the old man. He stared at his busy executioners with calm unwinking hatred, knowing that what was going to happen was inevitable, that there was no escape from it, as if he had been expecting that it would end this way all along.

Schulze drew himself up to his full height. He flashed a look at Schirmer. The latter gave a slight nod and tensed for the high-pitched burr of the machine-guns. Schulze swung round on his heel in a flurry of grey dust. '*Hab' acht!*' he commanded in a harsh dry bellow.

The birds rose in the skeletal trees that surrounded the fort with a hoarse croaked alarm. For a moment there was no sound but the soft beat of their wings, the startled birds flapping higher and higher into the burning, ominous sky, as if solely concerned with getting away from what was going to happen below.

'Gunners,' Schulze ordered, 'gunners – *take aim!*'

With the practised ease of the veterans that they were, the hard-faced young men squatting behind the machine-guns pulled back the cocking handles, not even hearing the desperate wails of the victims.

Schulze raised his right arm. Schirmer took a last look at the old man.

He was as erect and proud as ever. In death he alone had dignity, but it was a dignity steeled by an unquenching hatred. Suddenly Schirmer felt a trace of fear. Could they ever conquer that kind of hatred?

Next instant Schulze cried, '*FEUER!*'

The machine-guns burst into instant life, the gunners swinging them expertly from left to right and back again. The prisoners were galvanized into violent, hectic life, their skinny bodies ripped to bloody pulp at that range by a thousand bullets a minute.

'*Vive l'Algerie, vive* . . .' the old man's proud words were cut off suddenly as a sheet of slugs tore his stomach apart in a welter of red fury. He went down without another word . . .

FIVE

'The Boulevard of the Foreign Legion,' Schirmer announced grimly to his staff, as his weary Headhunters rose to their feet and prepared for another fifty minutes' slog through the burning heat. He pointed to the weathered column which testified that the rocky track ahead of them had been built by the men of the Legion back in the early part of the century. 'That's the start of it, erected by some humorist, long dead, I presume.'

'And so he should be,' White Lightning growled, pulling on his sixty pounds of equipment and staring at the great expanse of black gravel and rock flanked by bare rugged mountains that lay ahead of them, glittering in the merciless white rays of the desert sun. 'Christ, doesn't Mercier know I'm an American and Americans need wheels? They simply are not built for all this foot-slogging. We ain't got the feet for it.'

Petersen finished applying the last of his red nail varnish to the long nails of which he was inordinately proud, and simpered, 'But you've got some other – undoubtedly – more beautiful parts, darling, they tell me.'

'Yeah, what about my knuckles, Pansy?' he replied, doubling up his fist. 'I could let you have a nice knuckle sandwich here and now. I'm just in the right mood for it, old buddy.'

Pansy grinned, in no way put out. '*Liebchen*, you say the most wonderful things! No wonder I am in love with you.' He mouthed the sweating American struggling into his pack a wet kiss.

Schirmer grinned. The two of them were in good form, as

40

were the men. The Headhunters had borne up well under the strain of the long forced march from Colomb Bechar to Beni Abbes. It had been Colonel Mercier's idea to send them off without transport. He had said that it would appear that they were being punished for what he had called, with a knowing wink, their 'dastardly crime that had sullied the sweet name of *la belle France*'. Once they reached Beni Abbes, away from prying civilian eyes, they would be given transport, special trucks with balloon tyres adapted for desert travel. But first they had to reach the Legion fort.

Schirmer's grin disappeared. The terrain ahead was ideal for ambush and, besides, they were close to the ill-defined border with Morocco which raiders could easily cross if they so wished. No, he told himself, he would be glad when he had safely brought his men across the 'Boulevard of the Foreign Legion' to Beni Abbes. He beckoned to Schulze, who was cleaning his toenails with his bayonet.

The big NCO hobbled over to him. 'Sir?'

Schirmer lowered his voice, eyes surveying those grim black heights on both sides of the trail. 'Don't like the look of it, Schulze.'

Schulze, the veteran of six years of war with Wotan and all the years in the jungles of Indo-China, nodded his understanding. He tugged down his left eyelid. 'It's wooden eye, stay alert, sir, is it?'

'Exactly. I don't want the men alarmed, but pass the word back to the senior noncoms – discreetly – to keep their glassy orbits peeled.' He sniffed. 'It smells bad.'

'It's my feet, sir,' Schulze tried.

But Schirmer's face remained sombre. This afternoon he was suddenly not in the mood for jokes. Schulze hurriedly slipped into his para boot, slung his sixty pounds of equipment over his brawny shoulder as if it were nothing, and set off on his mission.

Schirmer raised his hand. The men tensed. He placed his whistle to his mouth and blew on it three times. '*Soldaten . . . eins, zwei, drei, vier . . .*'

The men wet their lips.

'*EIN LIED!*'

Picking up the slow deliberate pace of the Legion, they set off once more, singing that bold old marching song, which echoed a brutal pride in what they were and had once been in another war:

> '*Blow the bugle, beat the drum*
> *Clear the streets, here comes Wo-tan*
> *Steel is our weapon*
> *To hew through bone*
> *Blood our purpose*
> *Wotan hold close*
> *For Death is our Destiny . . .*'

Singing lustily at the head of his five hundred bold young men, Schirmer could not help but feel that this time that last line might well hold true . . .

Four hours later the weary Headhunters started to enter a defile, a grim narrow path in the black mountains beyond Fort Menouarar, their noncoms eyeing the crags on both sides apprehensively, as the shadows raced across the desert floor and started to ascend the heights. It would be pitch-black within the hour, for the desert night fell with startling suddenness.

'I've heard about this place, Colonel,' White Lightning, up at point with Schirmer, commented under his breath so that the others of the headquarters staff couldn't hear.

'What have you heard?' Schirmer asked grimly, wiping the sweat from his brow with the back of his hand.

'Nothing good,' White Lightning said, instinctively checking whether the safety was off on his machine-pistol.

'What's that supposed to mean?'

'This, sir. They once killed a general here. Back in 1928, General Clavery of the Legion and a party of his men were slaughtered here – *totally*. They ran into a raiding party – a *rezzou* – from over the border in Morocco. He was on his way to Beni Abbes too, sir.'

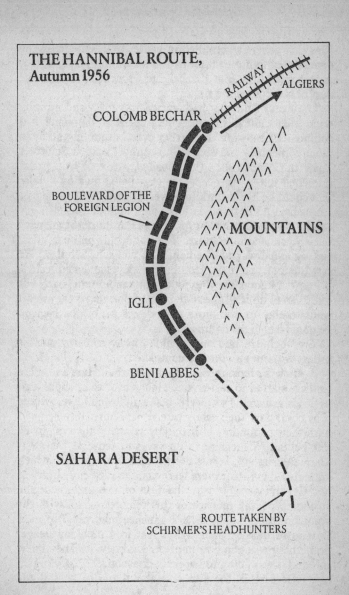

Schirmer looked at his second-in-command. 'Nice to hear that generals get killed in battle, too, sometimes,' he commented lightly, yet his eyes were sombre, and he, too, now began to look at the heights apprehensively, as the darkness crept up the slopes.

The heat of the day had started to vanish and a biting wind that chilled the marching men to the bone had commenced blowing. Now they were stumbling across a plain of pebbles and sharp flinty gravel, which Schirmer knew the Arabs called the *hammada*, or rocky desert. It crunched under their feet like egg-shells, making a noise that could be heard for kilometres. If there were raiders or ambushers up in those dark heights, he told himself, they would have heard the approaching Headhunters long ago.

He beckoned to Schulze. 'Put out scouts on both sides. Get them halfway up the heights if you can, Schulze.' He saw the look in the big Hamburger's eyes and said testily, 'I know, I know! They're not shitting mountain goats, but tell them to do it all the same. It's important, if they don't want to end up like those poor devils we buried back in Algiers forty-eight hours ago.'

'Sir,' Schulze said and doubled away to carry out his orders without any further comment.

By now the tension was almost tangible. Here and there soldiers started to cast anxious looks over their shoulders, as if they feared they were being followed. Everywhere they clicked off their safety catches and hurried to keep up with their comrades, as if they were afraid they might be left behind. Schirmer, as uneasy and tense as his men, knew their mood. It was not the fear of the known which animated them – for there were none so recklessly brave as his Headhunters. It was the fear of the unknown: the strange brooding menace of this remote ravine, with the wind howling down it like a banshee, churning up little flurries of dust at their weary feet in a mocking dance. Something was going to happen. He knew it. They knew it – and it was going to happen very soon.

It was just as the sun was about to slip behind the

mountains for good and plunge the tight ravine into the heavy darkness of the African night that Schirmer reluctantly made his decision. They would never reach the exit from the mountains by nightfall and his Headhunters were simply too tired to keep on marching all night. Besides, in the darkness stragglers could be picked off in ones and twos and he couldn't risk letting any of his men fall into the hands of the notoriously cruel and savage desert tribesmen alive. If they were to be attacked this night, he preferred it to be at a site of his own choice and with his Battalion at full strength.

'Halt the column, Major,' he commanded White Lightning and, stopping gratefully, relieved himself of his pack and heavy equipment while his weary, footsore Headhunters stumbled by.

The tall, handsome American, his face hollowed out to a death's head in the stark light, looked worried. 'We're tempting fate, sir,' he said gravely.

'Haven't we always?' Schirmer commented with a wry grin.

Speedily, his veterans set up camp, forming their shelter-halves into crude two-man tents; mixing sand and gasoline together into thick porridge in old cans, and igniting it in order to cook their evening rations on the blue flame; building rough barriers of camel thorn and rocks on both sides of the camp where it faced the mountains, to form rough defensive positions. Nodding his shaven head repeatedly in approval, an open can of hash in his hand, Schirmer moved through his busy men, patting a shoulder here, making a little joke there, constantly aware that somewhere up there in the darkness above, hard black eyes were watching the flickering gasoline fires and waiting. Then, apparently satisfied with what he had seen, he gave the orders to post sentries, and seemingly as an afterthought added, 'Oh and yes, Major, ensure that the fires are kept going all night. It's going to be damned cold up here and I don't want their outside plumbing freezing up. They are a rum bunch as it is.'

White Lightning looked at Schirmer, aghast. Bonfires would give away their positions for miles around; it was a standing invitation for any lurking enemy to attack. He opened his mouth to object and then grinned hugely.

Schirmer had his right eye closed in a mighty wink. The CO had some devilish scheme or other up his sleeve.

He snapped to attention with mock formality and barked in a voice that rose far and high in the still moutain air, 'At your command, sir!' All right, you non coms, don't stand around like wet farts waiting to hit the side of the thunderbox. Get those fires lit. You heard the CO didn't you . . .?'

'There . . .' Spider Arse began, but Schulze clamped his big paw around his mouth and stifled the words.

'I can see it, arse-with-ears,' he hissed. 'There's somebody up there.'

'What do you make of it, Schulze?' Schirmer asked softly, taking his gaze off the bonfires flickering a dull scarlet far below in the black sea of the ravine.

Schulze didn't answer for a moment. Instead he carried out the old desert trick of turning his head to one side, swinging it to the front with his gaze held tight to the ground. Suddenly he jerked his eyes up. Now everything loomed up a lighter black against the stark black of the moonless night.

'There looks to be three or four of them up there, sir,' he hissed. 'I don't think they're hitting the hay. Just lookouts probably, dozing on their feet.'

Schirmer absorbed the information and flashed a look at the green glowing dial of his wrist watch. It was nearly midnight. All was silent below, save for the odd noise of a sentry's boots on the rocks. His guess was that their unknown assailants would attack when the camp was sunk in the deepest sleep of all, the one that overcomes tired men around two in the morning. They'd know the habits of the Legion by now, with its traditional stand-to just before dawn

– which in these parts would be about four. Their attackers would reason they had two hours, therefore, to carry out their ambush. 'My guess is that they're the lookouts guarding the main body,' he whispered, 'perhaps bedded down till the time of the attack – behind the heights.'

There was a soft chorus of agreement from his raiding force, twenty men, all volunteers and all veterans of many raids of this kind in Indo-China. 'If we can get by them, sir,' Schulze hissed, 'we've got them with their dirty drawers around their skinny brown ankles, the lousy slopeheads.'

'I hope you're right,' Schirmer answered. 'But we can't waste any more time down here discussing it. All right,' he rose stiffly, and the others followed. 'We've got to get up that cliff first and we've got to do it without making any noise. I don't have to tell you if they catch us halfway up that climb, we'll be going home in wooden overcoats.'

'Or worse,' Spider Arse chimed in.

'Hold your water,' Schulze growled. 'You're a proper little bundle of joy, you are. Besides you ain't got as much to lose as I have.' He clutched the front of his trousers significantly, but no one laughed at his attempt at crude humour; they were all much too tense.

'*Los!*' Schirmer commanded, 'let's get on with it.' He picked up a handful of night-damp soil and rubbed it on his face. The others did the same. Without waiting for orders, they spread out below the steep climb and took up position. Schirmer reached up until he found his first handhold. 'Now,' he commanded.

It was every man for himself and Schirmer left his veterans to it as he concentrated on digging his toes into the sandy rock, edging his way upwards millimetre by millimetre, clinging till the ends of his fingers were numb with the strain and his powerful shoulder muscles were afire.

Despite the coldness of the night, the sweat broke out all over his body. In seconds he was drenched and had to toss his head from side to side at regular intervals to prevent the beads of perspiration from blinding him. Still he and the rest climbed on doggedly.

Six metres from the top he commenced working his way through a patch of murderous camel thorn bristling with vicious prongs, which ripped and tore at his flesh. More than once he hung there perilously, gasping for breath, unable to move for the thorns dug deep into his uniform. Furiously he twisted and turned in his attempts to release himself from the cruel barbs which held him prisoner, feeling them lashing across his face, drawing blood as he freed himself. Desperately, he bit his bottom lip to prevent himself from crying out with pain.

Slowly but surely, however, he and his men got ever closer to the summit, fighting the rock and the thorns with stubborn fury, as if they were live things. Schirmer was now within grasping distance of the ledge at the top. He reached up, searching for a handhold in the darkness, balancing on a flattish rock at his right foot. Suddenly it gave. He held on with his right hand, feeling the rock ripping off his nails, sending a wave of almost unbearable red-hot agony surging through his arm. He stifled his cry of pain just in time. Next moment he had clawed his way over the top and had dropped face-forward into the cropped, damp desert grass, shoulders heaving violently as if he had just run a great race.

Five minutes later, on legs that were strangely rubbery, the little group of Headhunters stole forward in the night like the killer wolves that they were. Down below in a small circular hollow they could just make out the black camel-hair tents of their unknown enemy. All was silent. No one had seen them. Before they could put their plan into action, they first had to deal with the lookouts they had spotted from below.

Followed by Schulze and Spider Arse, Schirmer crept towards the nearest lookout, head bent slightly as if he were dozing, outlined a stark black against the rock on which he rested. Now they were twenty metres away, crouched low below the level of his vision if he chanced to open his eyes . . . Fifteen metres . . . ten . . .

Schirmer thrust out his hands to left and right.

Schulze and Spider Arse reacted like well-trained veterans. In spite of the tension, Schirmer smiled grimly. He could always trust his 'old heads' in situations like this. He started to move forward again. Now he was almost within grabbing distance of the Arab. He began to prepare for the attack.

Abruptly the lookout started to open his eyes. Schirmer held his breath. One cry and the whole camp would be alarmed. Almost stupidly, Schulze looked at the dark figure crouched there in front of him. He opened his mouth to shout in the very same instant that Schulze's 'Hamburger Equalizer' flashed in the darkness. The Arab groaned softly as the vicious set of brass knuckles slammed into the side of his head, knocking him out. Schirmer's hands shot out to catch the sentry. He lowered the unconscious man to the ground almost lovingly. The rest of the Headhunters were dealing with the lookouts in time-honoured Legion fashion. Knives flashed, loaded sticks came swinging down, fingers found and latched on to skinny throats. In a matter of moments it was all over, and the Arabs lay sprawled out in the dust like broken, abandoned dolls.

Schirmer halted on the rim of the rocks overlooking the tented camp and made a quick calculation. Twenty tents with perhaps five men to a tent. One hundred of them against twenty! Then he told himself: They *were* the Headhunters . . . and the Headhunters always fought with the odds stacked against them. Mercier saw to that, he was very good at killing Boche. 'Schulze,' he hissed, 'you come in from the right flank with ten men . . . I'll come in from the left. Mps[1] and incendiary grenades. Don't attempt to get in any closer. I just want to knock out as many of the treacherous bastards as possible and then be off. By the time the rest of them – wherever they may be – have recovered, the Battalion will be on its way and out of these damned mountains. *Klar?*'

'*Klar*'.

'Then off you go.'

[1] Machine pistols.

'Good luck, sir.'

'And good luck to you, too, you big rogue. And watch yourself. Out of my pay, Schulze, I simply couldn't afford to pay for a Battalion booze-up if you snuffed it.'

'Try my best not to do so, sir,' Schulze whispered cheerfully and then he was gone.

Schirmer began to time him. He knew of old that in night ops like this timing was essential if he was going to prevent friend firing at friend. If the business was not controlled and timed exactly it could all end in chaos. 'All right,' he alerted his little command. 'The sergeant-major must be in position now.' He rose to his feet. '*Alles fuer Deutschland!*' he cried at the top of his voice.

From the other side of the camp, Schulze's deep bass boomed back, '*ALLES FUER DEUTSCHLAND!*'

Schirmer threw back his right hand. With a deep grunt, he flung his first grenade. It sailed hissing through the air, trailing fiery-red sparks behind. A soft whoosh. A dry crack. The incendiary exploded at the side of the nearest black tent in a flash of brilliant, blinding white light. In an instant night became day. Flames leapt up at once. Arabs came tumbling out, their robes on fire. Schirmer threw up his machine-pistol. Without appearing to aim, he fired a swift controlled burst from the hip. The Arabs slammed to the ground, arms and legs flailing, screaming piteously, as the steel ripped their skinny unprotected bodies apart.

Now grenades were sailing through the air from both sides. The helpless, panic-stricken tribesmen, ran to and fro, easy targets for the Headhunters, outlined as they were by the white glaring light. They hadn't a chance. It was not war; it was murder. The Headhunters mowed them down without mercy, faces set in a wolfish snarl as they pumped shot after shot into the trapped tribesmen.

Then it was all over. The tented camp was a bloodstained burning shambles of dead and dying men, scuffed sand, gleaming cartridge cases, the only sounds the moans and pleas of the dying. Schulze went from Arab to Arab, kicking them routinely, and when they groaned, placing the muzzle of his pistol behind their right ears and blowing the back of their heads off. The ambushers had been well and truly ambushed.

Thirty minutes later Schirmer's Headhunters were double-marching out of the mountains. Behind them on the Boulevard of the Legion, the contorted faces of the newly murdered men were already beginning to flush scarlet in the rays of the ascending sun. It was only when Schirmer finally felt satisfied that they were out of the ravines and allowed his gasping, sweat-lathered men a five minute break, that Schulze presented him with the new problem.

It came in the shape of a familiar weapon, once well-beloved by Schirmer's SS men on the Eastern Front. 'Why,' he exclaimed as Schulze handed the captured weapon to him, 'it's an old Schmeisser, Schulze!' He turned it over in admiration, 'And in perfect condition. Those slopeheads certainly knew how to take care of their weapons.'

Schulze stared at the weapon, while all around the hard-pressed Headhunters, their tunics black with sweat, gasped harshly for breath like ancient asthmatics. 'Don't think so, sir. Just have a look at the arsenal mark.'

Puzzled, Schirmer turned the weapon round to do as Schulze had requested. Stamped into the blue-black of the metal was the usual 'WH' of the *Wehrmacht*[1]. Nothing unusual in that, he told himself. What was the big rogue on about? He stopped short. 'Heaven, arse and cloudburst!' he exclaimed, *'the date!'*

'Exactly, sir.'

Schirmer looked at the big NCO, 'But how did a weapon like this – date of manufacture 1955, ten years *after* the German *Wehrmacht* disappeared from the face of the earth, come to land in this God-forsaken spot?'

'Mrs Schulze's handsome son', usually all-knowing, had no answer ready for that particular crucial question . . .

[1] Wartime German Army.

SIX

The *regibats*, tall impressive figures in their large blue turbans and light blue uniforms, snapped to attention and raised their gleaming sabres in salute, as Colonel Schirmer strode in out of the sun, followed by his staff, to pay his respects to Colonel Guy Comte de Gray, the commander of the Beni Abbes area.

Outside in the Scorpion Oasis the muezzin was calling the faithful to prayer and the desert Arabs were beginning to squat among their grumbling, grunting camels as the cry *'Allah ila la Allah'* was taken up and began to echo down the burning, white-bright valley.

Schirmer casually acknowledged the salute in the fashion of the Legion, while White Lightning whispered out of the side of his mouth, as the Count came forward to meet them, dressed in an expensive *burnoos*, wearing the same silken turban as his guards, 'Holy mackerel, Colonel! Get a load of his nibs. Ain't he just the fancy one?'

Schirmer nodded, not taking his eyes off the camp commandant, who was followed by a simpering, overly pretty orderly, who swished as he was walked behind his master. 'Very fancy indeed,' he said grimly. He knew the type. Headquarters back in Algiers was full of them. He stopped at the regulation six paces away from the tall slim Frenchman with the slanting green eyes, who outranked him by one star, and flung him an impressive salute. 'Schirmer, sir!' he bellowed so that the Count winced, as if in extreme pain, 'reporting in from Algiers, sir!'

Almost as an afterthought, the Count languidly raised

his riding crop to his turban, 'Ah the famous – or is it the *infamous*, Erwin Schirmer and his Headhunters, eh?'

White Lightning flushed – he was always very sensitive about the reputation of his bunch of renegade SS men. Schirmer's face did not change. Instead he said, 'Have it as you wish, sir. Yes, we're Mercier's Boche killers.'

Now it was the Count's turn to flush. The simpering orderly hastily rushed forward, as the flustered Count held out his hands. A little bottle appeared from out of the native's sleeve and poured something into the Count's palms. With a sigh of relief, the latter dabbed the liquid onto his face. Schirmer's nostrils were assailed with the sharp pungent odour of expensive eau-de-cologne. Behind him White Lightning's mouth dropped open stupidly. He had never seen a soldier parade his deviation so openly.

The Count did not seem to notice. He said, 'Be so good as to follow me. I have been informed by Higher Head-quarters that I must assist you.' Without another word, he turned and walked with an affected gait deeper down the dark stone corridor.

Pansy Petersen nudged White Lightning knowingly and breathed, 'Get me the vaseline, darling. I could follow a lovely honey-bun like that to the end of the earth!'

'What's this,' Schulze exclaimed, thrusting the little camouflage cap to the back of his big shaven blond head, 'the feeding of the frigging five thousand?'

He paused at the sight of the crowd of garrison troops milling around the soup kettles, attended to by grumpy elderly cooks stripped to the waist and running with sweat, as the men, native and French, clamoured for their breakfast. 'You can't expect a senior NCO to line up for his vittels with that shitting mob.'

Next to him, Spider Arse grinned. Schulze turned on him immediately. 'And what have you to grin about, you asparagus Tarzan, you!' he snorted.

'A lot,' the other NCO replied cheerfully, a roguish look

on his face. 'I know where there's better fodder to be had than a canteen of lukewarm nigger sweat, and goulash made of old nags from the knacker's yard.' He lowered his voice and winked significantly, 'And all served by real live female gash!'

Schulze's mouth dropped open in unfeigned amazement and he almost let his canteen fall into the sand. 'Did you say real live – *female*-gash?' he repeated in a hoarse, unbelieving whisper. 'I thought all they had in this place was those rotten camels,' he indicated the beasts squatting in the oasis below.

'I did, Sarnt-Major,' Spider Arse answered confidently, 'but of course, for a consideration, a gift of love, you might say.' He laughed coarsely and made the German gesture of counting money with his finger and thumb.

'But where does the gash come from in this God-forsaken dump? I mean . . .'

Spider Arse hastily drew him to one side so that he couldn't be heard by the others. 'Keep it down to a dull roar, Sarnt-Major, for Chrissake!' he appealed. 'It's them slopeheads with the silk knickers on their turnips,' he indicated Colonel de Gray's *regibats*. 'That honey-bun of a CO of theirs has set up a nice little knocking shop for them down in the oasis when they're off duty, so that they can get the dirty water off their chests regular like and not bother the Arabs' camels.'

Shrewdly Schulze looked down at a knowing Spider Arse and then at the camp commandant's own personal guards. The *regibats* were tall, very handsome men, but there was something particularly ruthless about their dark eyes. Schulze shivered involuntarily. 'That lot look as if they'd whip off yer outside plumbing with them big penknives of theirs without as much as a by your leave,' he said doubtfully.

Spider Arse laughed easily. 'Don't cream yer skivvies, Sarnt-Major. They only go to visit the gash at night after duty. The gash is bored stiff all day long, only too eager to get slipped a nice piece of hard German sausage. Now then, Sarnt-Major, if you and me could get themsens sent off on a little reconnaissance mission for the next two or three hours – perhaps sounding out the slopeheads down there about the desert? – I could well imagine that we'd be having something better than nigger-sweat and giddi-up goulash for breakfast, eh?'

Schulze's brick-red face lit up, all doubts cast to the winds. 'By God and all his Great Red Triangles, you're an ugly little shit, Spider Arse, but I must admit that you've got something else than cold gravy in yer noddle.' He raised his right leg and gave one of his classical triumphant farts that set the camels squatting down below off grumbling once more. 'What are we waiting for, you perverted banana-sucker. Lead on. Let's get at that lovely grub!'

'This area is called the "*erg cheche*",' Colonel Comte de Gray lectured the listening Headhunters, while the fan whirred softly above their cropped heads and the simpering orderly stood by with his scent at the ready. 'That means the region of the sand storms. Surprisingly enough, it is rich in plant life. So we conclude that there is water there, though some of the plants have roots five metres deep, and the tamarisks, which look like shrubs, but are really trees, have roots going down twenty-five metres.'

'So you conclude, Colonel,' Schirmer interrupted him impatiently, 'that there is water there and that Hannibal's route could have led through that direction.'

The Count frowned, then nodded. 'Yes. So if we agree on that, we advance still further into the desert to this area,' he indicated a large white space on the map, with a few vague features entered on it. 'Here we have the red sandstone formation which Colonel Mercier has told you about. There, according to what little we know of the area, there is little vegetation and infrequent sandstorms, but to all intents and purposes it is too inhospitable to shelter human life.'

Schirmer stepped over to the map and measured the distances and angles with his outstretched hands, while the others watched and awaited his decision. 'Well, Colonel,' he said finally, stepping back, 'if there is anything to this Hannibal route business, logically the trail would lead through that red sandstone area into the *erg cheche*, on to Beni Abbes and from thence to the coast.' He watched the Count's weakly handsome aristocratic face for some reaction, but there was none. Colonel Comte de Gray, he realized, didn't care one way or other. He had already sold out – mentally – to the rebels. He would serve out his time here in Beni Abbes with his colourful guards and faithful boy; then when the French Army was finally kicked out of Algeria, he would retire to his estates, wherever they might be, travelling up to Paris at monthly intervals to pick up the perverts at the Gare d'Austerlitz until he became too old to be interested in such things any more.

He moved away from the map. 'Well, Colonel, what can you offer us in way of transport?' Schirmer asked in a cold, matter-of-fact tone.

For the first time since they had entered the office, the Headhunters got a reaction out of the Count, other than that of well-bred distaste. 'You mean, you are prepared to go through with this, Schirmer?' he asked, disbelief evident in his careful, upper-class voice.

'Of course, sir.'

'But I thought it was just another of Mercier's mad schemes. Something for him to make his mark at Algiers Headquarters. All those people up there live for is promotion.'

Schirmer said nothing.

'But surely you realize just how mad his scheme is?' the Count persisted, a note of pleading beneath the aristocratic veneer now. 'We don't even know if the Hannibal route ever existed, and even if it did, there is no evidence that this Red Oasis was along it. Besides, there are thousands of square miles of unexplored territory out there. You could spend months searching it. There are . . .'

Schirmer still said nothing, though his mind was racing. Why was the Count becoming so agitated, he asked himself? The man seemed above the concerns of ordinary mortals. Yet now his aristocratic pose was crumbling rapidly.

Finally Schirmer had had enough. He broke into the

Count's protests with a harsh, 'But you have the transport as promised, Colonel?'

The Count took a deep breath, his eyes taking in Schirmer's hard, scarred face, as if he were seeing him for the very first time. 'Yes,' he said slowly, 'I've got the transport. The usual Trans-Sahara balloon tyre trucks.'

'Excellent, sir, thank you,' Schirmer snapped promptly, still wondering why the Count was suddenly so concerned about his mission. 'Then, with your permission, sir, I shall withdraw. We have a great number of preparations to make before . . .'

'Sir.' It was Pansy Petersen. He held up the bundle he was carrying – significantly.

'Oh, yes, *Leutnant.*' He suddenly recalled he had asked Petersen to remind him in case he forgot. He accepted the bundle from the other officer and unwrapped it swiftly to reveal the Schmeisser that Schulze had taken from the dead rebel after the abortive ambush attempt.

The Count stared down at it. 'Well?' he demanded.

'We took it from a group of tribesmen who attempted to jump us back on the Boulevard of the Foreign Legion, sir,' Schirmer explained swiftly.

'So, what is remarkable about it? It is one of those lethal gadgets which you Germans seem to excel at manufacturing,' the Count said, not able to withstand the dig. 'Taken from some dump set up by Rommel, I suppose.'

'I know, sir. But there is something strange about this particular – er – lethal gadget. It appears to have been manufactured *ten years after Herr Hitler and Co went out of business!*'

'What did you say?'

Grimly, Schirmer repeated his statement, not taking his eyes off the face which had become a shade paler. The Colonel's boy offered him the eau-de-Cologne and he dabbed it on his brow hastily with none of his previous affectation.

Schirmer waited and then he said, 'I don't suppose you could give me an explanation, sir?'

Comte de Gray lowered his gaze before those hard, piercing bright blue eyes. 'No,' he said without conviction, 'I'm afraid, I can't.'

Schirmer instinctively knew the man was lying. He touched his hand to his cap in salute. 'Then we'll get on to that transport, sir,' he said coldly. 'Good morning.'

'Good morning,' the other man answered, returning the salute.

Schirmer noted that the Count's hand was trembling. Something strange was going on here at Beni Abbes, but for the life of him, he could not make out what.

'*Hit the dirt* – for God's sake!' Schulze hissed urgently. He gave the happily grinning NCO next to him a mighty shove.

Spider Arse slammed into the grove of palms just behind the hut inhabited by the native whores. 'What the hell's going on—'

Schulze's big paw clamped down hard over his mouth as the sergeant-major dived to the ground next to him and cut off the rest of his startled question.

Not releasing his grip, he whispered, 'Cast your glassy orbits on that.' He indicated the group of Colonel de Gray's *regibats* striding purposefully through the native section of the oasis.

'Holy strawsack!' Spider Arse groaned, 'it's them! Do you think they've tumbled us? I mean it was really lovely grub . . . like dipping it in warm olive oil, but I don't think it's worth—'

'They'll tumble us for sure, if you go on shooting off your mouth like that. Hold yer water and let's have a see.' Cautiously, Schulze pulled out his Hamburger Equalizer and slipped the brass knuckles on his right fist. It was the only weapon he possessed just then and Colonel de Gray's men were all clearly heavily armed.

But Schulze's caution was unwarranted. The *regibats* were not interested in the whores and the fact that the 'white faces' had been carving themselves a slice of that particular fruit cake this morning. They strode purposefully to where a group of desert Arabs were squatting on their haunches around a flickering fire of dried camel dung, moodily sipping green tea and smoking fitfully. They squatted with them and started to talk excitedly, using a large number of forceful gestures, time and time again indicating the unknown desert beyond the Scorpion Oasis. Finally the Arabs started to nod, as if agreeing to something. Hidden in the palms, the two watchers saw how money changed hands and the Arabs began to saddle their camels.

Ten minutes later they were gone, cantering off into the burning sand sea, watched by the *regibats* until they had disappeared from sight in the blue, shimmering haze of the mid-morning. Then, and only then, did the camp commandant's soldiers return to their quarters, leaving the two NCOs to stare at each other in bewilderment.

'Now what do you make of that, Spider Arse?' Schulze broke the heavy brooding silence, rising to his feet slowly and beginning to brush the sand from his knees. 'What in three devils' names is so important as to get them slopeheads riding off into the desert?'

'And what have those shits in the blue knickers got to do with them?' his companion added his own puzzled question. 'They gave them a bunch of Marie, as well.[1] Why?'

Schulze shook his head. 'How should I know, plush ears, I ain't Jesus, yer know? But it's funny, very funny.' He dismissed the matter. 'Well, come on, you've had yer little bit of fun – and in your case, it was very little indeed,' he added with a sneer. 'Let's get back to the Headhunters.'

'*Little!*' Spider Arse exclaimed vehemently. 'Little indeed! Why do you think I've got these here round shoulders and a hoarse voice like I have, eh? It's 'cos of the weight of my dong, dragging at me vocal chords, that's why.'

Laughing uproariously, the two running-mates staggered off back to their Battalion. Behind them the desert burned and waited . . .

[1] Marie: SS slang for money.

SEVEN

The next twenty-four hours at Beni Abbes flew by, while the Headhunters prepared their trucks, with their great balloon tyres and half-tracks, for the long trek ahead of them. There were a hundred and one problems to be solved, and Schirmer and his officers were kept on their toes attending to them, as the half-naked Headhunters, many of them clad only in their jock-straps, sweated over engines and suspensions.

Schirmer, his face brick-red and constantly lathered in sweat, came to loathe the burning red ball of the sun which hung in the sky all day long and beat down on him relentlessly. Even in the patches of shade cast by the dusty palms, there was no escaping that murderous heat and he thought longingly of the sea back at Algiers. How delightful it would be to slip into its cooling blue water and escape from these burning sands and the stiffling opaque haze hanging over the shimmering desert!

In the cool of the first evening, Schirmer personally took out one of the vintage Citroen half-tracks to test its performance in the desert. He found himself wincing with shock every time his flesh came into contact with the metal parts which were still red-hot from the day's sun, breathing a sigh of heartfelt relief when he eventually managed to get the cumbersome heavy truck into first gear, and a faint breeze started to drive away the relentless stifling heat.

Pushing his foot down hard, he drove the shaking vehicle full-out, scattering the jerboas, the desert rats, by the score as they bounded away in terror on their long hind legs, like little kangaroos. Now, as the dark velvet of the African night rapidly began to sweep across the desert, the eyes of unknown animals began to glint out of the flying darkness and, even above the rattle of the truck, he could hear rustlings and slitherings as though something was stalking him. Colonel Schirmer quickly dismissed the thought, telling himself that the desert was going to take some getting used to, for him and his Headhunters.

It was just then that he spotted the ring of fires directly ahead. He made a quick decision. He had no option but to charge through the fires in case it was another ambush. But when he came abreast of them, he found there was no one there; the fires, built of camel thorn and desert scrub, were burning by themselves, completely untended.

Colonel Schirmer braked to a stop, keeping his foot on the accelerator, gunning the engine, clutch depressed for a hasty start, and loosened his pistol in its holster. He strained his eyes in the glowing darkness. There was no one in sight, but just next to the nearest fire he could see scuffed sand and the imprint of naked feet. Someone had been there quite recently for the fires were still burning brightly. But who had they been, and what had they been doing out here in the sandy waste? Were they shepherds perhaps, who had lit the fires to warm them through the bitingly cold desert night? But if that was the case, where were they now? Surely he would be able to hear the bleating of their flocks? And if they weren't shepherds, who were they? Suddenly he felt an icy finger of fear trace its way down his spine, and abruptly the short hairs at the back of his skull stood erect. An eerie sensation flooded over him that he was being watched. Cursing himself for being an unreasoning fool, he let out the clutch and hit the accelerator. The big truck lurched forward. Next moment Colonel Schirmer was racing recklessly across the desert at full speed back to Beni Abbes, as if the devil himself were after him. Behind him, the night finally settled down over the Sahara, hiding who or whatever lay out there. Schirmer didn't look back . . .

*

On the following morning, Schirmer and his officers supervised the loading of supplies, the big German colonel personally checking the load in each individual vehicle; for he knew just how important it was to ensure that everything was there. The officers ticked off every single item. A mistake in the number of jerricans of water, or even insufficient salt tablets, so vital in the intense heat of the daytime, could spell disaster. They slowly worked their way down the long lists, which even contained items such as fruit salts to make the stale water in the jerricans drinkable. Then came the weapons and ammunition, each man being restricted to his automatic or machine-pistol, grenades (three), and two hundred pounds of 9 mm. Schirmer did not like the quotas he had imposed himself, particularly the fact that he was leaving behind most of the Headhunters' heavy machine-guns and mortars; but he knew that water and gas were perhaps more important than firepower on a trek like this. As he confided in an equally worried White Lightning, 'If, and I repeat *if*, we run into trouble out there, I'm taking a calculated risk that the desert Arabs will be armed with those antiquated rifles of their own and whatever military cast-offs they have been able to acquire since World War Two.'

'You're rather forgetting that Schmeisser, sir,' White Lightning reminded him, wiping the dripping beads of sweat from his forehead.

But Colonel Schirmer did not seem to hear him.

By midday the long task was completed and Schirmer sprang his surprise on his sweat-drenched, dehydrated Headhunters. From the Scorpion Oasis came a long line of native women, bearing steaming dishes, followed by men with kettles of green tea and mint, and two of Colonel de Gray's native guard staggering under the weight of a huge metal cask.

Schulze's mouth dropped open stupidly when he spotted the cask and in a faint voice, he whispered to Spider Arse, 'Pinch me, comrade, go on . . . It can't be . . . But if my eyes don't deceive me, that's – *BEER!*'

'What?' Spider Arse exclaimed. 'Did you say *suds!*'

'I certainly did – and it ain't no mirage. Real pissy beer!' Suddenly his expression changed and he added gloomily, 'You know what the Old Man's up to, don't yer?'

'What?'

'He's fattening us up for the kill,' Schulze replied sombrely, as the native women started to dole out huge portions of steaming couscous into the canteens of waiting Headhunters, their faces wreathed in happy smiles.

'The shitting prisoner ate a shitting hearty breakfast?' Spider Arse said.

'Exactly.'

A hundred metres away . . . elegant quarters decorated with the trophies and souvenirs of half a lifetime spent in Africa, Colonel de Gray also served his guests, Schirmer and his officers. He placed before them a great chafing-dish full of couscous, piled high with the basic ground wheat, in which were entombed half a dozen scraggy, bald-necked desert chickens, all served with scorchingly hot, highly spiced sauces which would take the roof off the mouth of the unwary, who mistook them for some kind of ketchup. Meanwhile his orderly made a great fuss with the bottles of imported white wine, which his master had opened specially for his guests, though most of them would have preferred the cheap Algerian beer being enjoyed by their thirsty soldiers.

The Frenchman ceremoniously handed Schirmer the sheep's eyes which had been glaring at him from the steaming mix and Schirmer solemnly accepted the two titbits and swallowed them whole, as was the custom.

The officer smirked at Schirmer and said, 'So this night you leave, Colonel Schirmer? What are your feelings setting off into the unknown like this?'

Schirmer looked at the pale-faced, aristocratic Frenchman, trying to see behind the polite smile and the dead eyes, and failing to do so. 'I could say I feel like a horse's arse, Colonel!' he answered crudely. 'But I tell myself I am a professional soldier and must answer what all professional soldiers answer on such occasions. It is my duty – and I must do it.'

'Duty?' the Count mused, pressing his elegantly manicured fingers together pensively. 'But you are a German . . . a mercenary, if I may be bold enough to say so. What duty have you to France?'

'*Not* to France, Colonel, but to myself, my soldiers and – perhaps – to the cause of Europe.'

The Count laughed politely and suddenly held his hand in front of his mouth, as if he did not wish to reveal his teeth to his guest. 'The cause of Europe – *out here!* But, my dear fellow, however did you come to have such *drôle* ideas?'

Schirmer looked hard at the French Colonel. '*Drôle ideas* – how did I come by them?' he echoed. 'Three years in Russia, four in Indo-China, Colonel, I think that should suffice.' He leaned forward, eyes gleaming in sudden anger. 'Someone must stop the rot, even if it is low creatures such as Colonel Mercier's tame Boche,' he hissed. 'For us it is *march or croak, Colonel!*'

Colonel de Gray was taken aback by such naked hatred. He hastily beckoned to his orderly, who started to pour the wine immediately. The rest of the meal was eaten in silence.

Afterwards when his guests had gone and Hassan, the orderly, was busy preparing his opium pipe for the afternoon, Colonel Comte de Gray sat in his big cane chair, staring out at the shimmering blue waves of the desert, trying to fight off the feelings of shame precipitated by the big German's outburst. He was worried by what he had done. Suddenly, he realized with the clarity of a vision, after years of self-indulgence and absolute selfishness, that he was a traitor; that he had been one for years; and that those noisy Germans down below, busy preparing for their trek into the unknown, were unwittingly going to their death – because of him. Abruptly the tall, pale aristocrat buried his head in his hands and began to sob . . .

*

It was just before dawn and as yet the red disc of the new day's sun had not nudged its way across the velvet-black horizon. Outside the fort the desert was still clothed in an inky-black darkness, the only sound the soft shuffle of the sentries in the dust and the tired little noises that men make when they are half-awake.

Schirmer was standing next to the lead truck, smoking fitfully, while his companion, White Lightning, muffled in a heavy goat-skin cloak, stared out at the desert. 'Penny for them, Colonel?' he asked softly after a while.

Schirmer smiled softly at the phrase. The big American had translated the expression literally from English into German, but he guessed at what White Lightning meant. 'Oh, not much, Major. Just running over the details in my head – things that have to be done today – that's all.'

'What do you think our chances are of finding this Red Oasis and stopping the situation degenerating out here?'

Schirmer considered for a moment, then he said, 'Oh let's worry about that later when the time is more opportune. At this moment my first concern is getting the show on the road and out of here before the slopeheads down there in the oasis are awake and about. The less they know about our movements, the better, in my opinion.'

'I suppose you're right, sir,' White Lightning said, straightening up and throwing away his butt in a red gleaming arc into the sand. 'Better get on with it then. Shall I order them to roll the trucks?'

'Yes, please do, Major,' Schirmer said with sudden formality, as if the occasion demanded it.

White Lightning clicked to attention and saluted. Then he was gone, leaving Schirmer alone for a few moments in the icy pre-dawn air, hardly aware, it seemed, that he was shivering with cold – or something.

They were off on their mission at last and at this moment it seemed nothing short of impossible: trying to find an oasis that might not be there in the middle of thousands of square kilometres of uncharted desert, with only themselves to rely on, a bunch of mercenaries who were obviously expendable. This was going to be the toughest assignment ever for his bunch of rogues and renegades.

Suddenly the first truck engine burst into life with a thick asthmatic cough, setting the half-starved dogs down in the oasis barking hoarsely. It was followed by engine after engine. Abruptly the air was filled with acrid blue gasoline fumes. Men tossed away their cigarettes. Rough voices gave brisk commands. Here and there, men cursed as they stumbled in the half darkness, but one after another, trucks filled up.

Schirmer took one last look at the fort. Strangely enough, a yellow light glowed in Colonel de Gray's office, in spite of the early hour. Idly he wondered why then, tossing away his own cigarette, he swung himself easily into the cab of the lead truck next to Sergeant-Major Schulze. 'All right,' he cried above the racket, remembering the good old days when they had first rolled so triumphantly into Russia in the summer of 1941, '*Carbide!*'

Schulze grinned mightily at the word. Obviously it brought back memories for him, too. He gave the driver a nudge in his skinny ribs that almost sent him flying out of the open cab, 'All right, tiger-turd, you heard the CO, didn't you. Roll em! *Carbide!*'

The driver hit the gas. The truck groaned. Slowly, it began to rumble forward, picking up speed by the second. Taking their cue truck after truck, all heavily laden with men and equipment, did the same. They were on their way. Schirmer's Headhunters were off into the unknown once again. Thirty minutes later the desert had swallowed them up and back at Colonel de Gray's office the yellow light went out . . .

INTO THE DESERT

'If you've knocked a nigger edgeways when e's thrustin' for
your life.
You must leave 'im very careful where 'e fell
An' may thank your stars an' gaiters if you didn't feel 'is
knife.'

R. Kipling: *Loot*

ONE

The first day was easy. The track, obviously the product of many centuries of bare feet and camel-hooves, was firm and hard. From time to time their progress southwards was slowed by patches of drifting sand from the *erg cheche*, and the long convoy was able to maintain a steady speed of twenty kilometres an hour throughout the daylight hours.

But if the track proved that tribesmen had been passing this way for years, the desert itself was empty, bare of anything but stunted vegetation and the occasional white-bleached bones of some dead animal or other. Schirmer, a khaki handkerchief knotted around his neck to soak up the sweat that constantly ran down his glistening face, told himself they could have been the last men on earth. The glowing brown wilderness was absolutely, completely deserted. Nevertheless he maintained strict march discipline, with sentries posted at every stop and grumbling Headhunters being forced to climb the nearest heights to survey the terrain ahead for any sign of trouble.

On the second day, the *erg cheche* showed its bad side. There had obviously been recent sand storms in the area they were now passing through and the going became soft and treacherous. An icy wind blew up, flinging particles of sand like bitter sharp knives against their brick-red faces. The men were glad of their thick greatcoats, as they laboured across dune after dune, which continued as far as the eye could see. Some of the dunes were gentle and rolling, but most were steep and razor-backed, and it took all the drivers' skill to tackle them. They would position their big trucks horizontally to the dune, accelerate at top speed and then, shortly before swooping over the top – perhaps to face a drop of ten metres or more – they would swing the wheel round violently and roll down the opposite side of the dune at a hair-raising angle. As Schulze commented more than once, face suddenly an ashen white, 'Great crap on the Christmas tree, it's up and down like a shitting jo-jo! I've spilled my cookies once again!'

But it was not only the razor-backed dunes that the tired, angry drivers had to contend with that day. There were also the patches of soft sand everywhere, which bogged down the heavily-laden trucks time and time again. Then everyone went over the side, grabbed a shovel and a length of metal track and set about the back-breaking time-consuming business of digging the stalled truck out, so that the metal sand channels could be placed under the wheels and the truck started once again.

By nightfall on that second day, they had had enough. The sand particles were everywhere, in spite of their goggles and face cloths, in their mouths, ears, eyes, nostrils, all over their bodies – so that they scratched themselves raw. Most of the bone-weary Headhunters flung themselves down to the ground and fell asleep immediately, too tired to start the gasoline-and-sand fires to cook their evening meal. For the first hours of that particular night, officers and senior NCOs were forced to do sentry duty while the exhausted soldiers slept.

For a while Schirmer reminisced with Schulze about the old days, their voices strangely hushed, as if they were awed by the immense spread of the night sky, studded with the bright cold silver of the stars. Finally Schirmer excused himself and returned to his bedroll underneath the lead truck.

But the big colonel found he could not sleep in spite of his exhaustion. While his men snored softly all around him, he lay on his back, hands propped underneath his head, staring at the unwinking stars, so close that it seemed he could reach up and pull one down, listening to the singing of the sand beyond. That strange melody given off by a million particles of sand contracting with the night cold and rubbing against each other. It was an eerie melody, yet somehow soothing and restful. Suddenly Schirmer sat up. Another more familiar sound had assailed his eardrums. A loud gurgling noise like bathwater running down into a drain. He frowned. He knew how it was produced, and by what.

A camel! Every now and again the awkward beast would puff out the side of its mouth in a fleshy balloon like an Ami chewing gum, accompanying the movement with an unpleasant bubbling sound. Most veterans of the Legion knew that this was the time to give a camel a wide berth; for at this moment it was particularly nasty to be bitten by the septic mouth of the snorting, sneering ugly creature.

Suddenly the full impact of the sound penetrated his sleepy brain. If there was a camel out there, there would be a rider, too. He hastily slipped on his boots on account of the scorpions and grabbed for his pistol.

Automatically, the ever-loyal Schulze lying at his side, huddled in his sleeping bag, cocked open one eye and said drily, 'Trouble sir?'

'Don't know.' Schirmer got to his feet. 'Come on.'

Schulze needed no second invitation. With surprising speed for such a big man, he thrust his feet into his desert boots and seized his machine-pistol. 'Which way, sir?' he hissed.

'Over there.' Schirmer indicated another of the razor-back dunes, shimmering an icy silver in the stars. 'Thought I heard camels out beyond it.'

Schulze whistled softly between his teeth. 'That means this place ain't the arsehole of the world after all, sir.'

'Looks like it,' Schirmer answered laconically, as the two of them stole forward, placing their feet down with exceeding care, the faint sounds they made covered by the night breeze. They reached the base of the dune, which was some twenty metres high and concealed whoever might be behind it from sight of the tented camp. Waving his automatic, Schirmer indicated that Schulze should move slightly to the right and then start to climb the dune. Schulze nodded his understanding and crept off. Schirmer waited an instant and then began to ascend the dune, body crouched intently, finger curled around the trigger of his pistol, lifting his feet cautiously so as not to make too much noise in the ankle-deep sand.

Now he could smell the fetid, choking, rancid smell of camels and hear them blowing out the sides of their mouths so that they bulged like a small boy blowing bubble-gum. He frowned, but did not cease climbing. There were more than one of them out there. Of course they could be harmless nomads, but if they were, why did they not approach the Headhunters? Hospitality was cherished in the desert where tribesmen might not see a stranger for months, even years. No, whoever was on the other side of the dune was definitely hostile or had something to hide.

Now he was just below the top of the dune. He threw a glance to his right. Schulze was in position too and waiting. He held up three fingers. Schulze nodded that he understood. Noiselessly, Schirmer counted off the seconds and cried at the top of his voice: '*NOW!*'

Next instant he flung himself over the top, pistol clutched firmly to his right hip.

There were three of them. Desert Arabs, two slumped on the seats of their camels, the other holding his beast by the head.

'*Lizards!*' the one holding the camel cried in French and dived for the pistol strapped to his waist.

Schirmer's automatic barked. The man screamed and dropped to one knee, a sudden flower of scarlet erupting on the chest of his dirty robe. He started to sway frighteningly.

To Schirmer's right, Schulze fired a quick burst. It went short. Sand spurted up in a swift, vicious line in front of the two mounted men. Their camels started violently. Schulze cursed and ducked the next moment as the first mounted Arab raised his weapon. The night air was sliced by the frenzied chatter of white tracer. Schulze flung himself to the ground, just in time, for a lethal hail of 9mm slugs hissed inches above his head.

Schirmer fired. The man who had fired at Schulze howled in absolute agony as the bullet slammed into his shoulder. Bright red blood jetted from the wound instantly and he let his weapon fall into the sand, his arm shattered.

Next moment a dark object sailed through the air towards the two Headhunters. '*Grenade!*' Schirmer shrieked in sudden alarm. '*Hit the dirt!*'

He and Schulze immediately flung themselves full-length in the sand. The grenade fell short and landed next to the third camel which reared high in the air with terror. Seconds later, the grenade exploded in a vicious red ball of flame. Razor-sharp splinters of steel whirled through the air. The camel went down, its ugly ungainly body ripped to shreds, rolling its dark eyes in its death throes, to tumble over and crush the wounded Arab.

That did it. The other Arabs dug their heels into the sides of their camels. As Schulze and Schirmer rose to their feet, firing as they did so, they were off, their camels going full out, robes flying, bodies low to escape the hail of bullets. Within minutes they were out of range of the two Headhunters' handfire weapons, and in the end Schirmer lowered his pistol and cried, 'All right, Schulze, cease fire . . . cease fire!' He cocked his head in the direction of the camp where whistles were already beginning to shrill and angry puzzled voices were calling out. 'They're creaming their skivvies down there.'

'Bunch of warm brothers,' Schulze growled, angry that the other two had got away. 'Piss down their legs at the first smell of powder!'

Schirmer grinned and then recalled the Arab trapped beneath the dying camel, writhing in the blood-red sand in its dying agony. 'All right, Schulze, I'll stay here. Get Tod and a couple of men. We'll see what we can find out from the one we've got.'

'Sir,' Schulze began and stopped short, as he spotted the weapon dropped by the Arab whom Schirmer had wounded in the shoulder. He picked it up and held it high so that the colonel could see it in the light of the stars. 'One thing we won't need that torturing little bastard for – is this, eh, sir?'

Schirmer's grin of triumph vanished. He nodded grimly as he recognized the old familiar shape of the Schmeisser. 'Yes,' he agreed, 'that we won't . . .'

The next morning dawned furnace-hot. As the column set off once again, with Tod waiting anxiously for their prisoner to recover consciousness, the sky above them was the bronze-brown of wood smoke. Not a breath of wind stirred. As the Citroens bumped and jolted their way across the rough surface of the desert, Schirmer shaded his eyes and stared upwards. The sun was like a coin glimpsed dimly at the bottom of a dirty pool. He shuddered a little, in spite of the sticky heat. He knew the signs. Trouble was brewing.

Hour after hour they progressed at a snail's pace over that barren lunar landscape, littered with huge boulders, zig-zagging all the time, the drivers cursing and sweating, their faces caked with white dust, their eyes red-rimmed with the strain. All the while, Schirmer kept throwing apprehensive glances at the burning sky.

'Sand storm?' White Lightning asked finally, putting Schirmer's own gloomy prediction into words.

Schirmer nodded. 'Think, so, Major. All the signs are there.'

White Lightning licked his sun-cracked lips and Schirmer could see that the last days in the desert had already begun to take their toll. Like the faces of the rest of the Headhunters, White Lightning's was leaner, his lips drawn fine, his eyes red, but hard and keen. They all looked like desert veterans. 'What's the drill, sir?' he asked after a while, wiping the sweat from around his neck with his sweat-rag.

'There's not much we can do but stop, crowd together for security – and,' he laughed drily, 'for those of our rogues who still believe in such mumbo-jumbo and bone-rattling, *pray!*'

One hour later it started. Abruptly the sun vanished and within seconds it started to grow as dark as night. A wind came from nowhere, growing in force by the second. Now the trucks were shuddering violently as they were struck by gust after stronger gust.

Schirmer bit his lip. This was it, he told himself, as he raised his hand so that the drivers behind could see him while there was still time, trying to ignore the flying particles of sand which were hitting his face like angry red-hot hail-stones.

Hastily the trucks started to close up, forming a rough circle, while excited and apprehensive Headhunters shouted to each other, the words snatched from their mouths in that whirling hectic bedlam of flying sand, vanishing from sight one by one, as the storm increased in fury by the second. Then, with engines stopped, the men holding on to whatever they could grab for dear life, the hot fetid wind struck them at a hundred kilometres an hour, buffeting their cringing bodies with lethal ferocity. Sand particles jetted through their thin uniforms. They howled with pain, but the wind ripped the cries from their gasping mouths and filled their lungs with sand. Breathing became difficult. The howling, hellish fog of sand grabbed the air from the men's breasts. They coughed and choked like asthmatics in their death throes.

On and on that great wind raged. Its ululating threnody rose to an ever louder pitch. It threatened to burst the cringing, whimpering men's eardrums at any moment. For two thousand kilometres it had travelled across the Sahara to seize them – and it was not to be cheated of its victims. Time and time again, it battered the puny little mortals with its hot clammy fist and they hung on to each other in frantic fear.

Once, in a brief pause, Schirmer rubbed the caked sand from his goggles and peered around him at the crouching, quaking men in his truck. Beyond them he could see nothing but flying sand. For all he knew, they were alone in this crazy, anarchic, howling world. He ducked his head again fearfully, as the sand storm came racing back. The wind shrieked and wailed with renewed fury, howling across the desert at a tremendous rate, as if some God on high had ordained that these mortals should be wiped from the face of the earth as punishment for their temerity in penetrating this wild secret place.

Abruptly the wind started to fall off. The maddening, never-ending howl was replaced by a soft, ever-decreasing dirge. This in turn gave way to a gentle hiss. Then it vanished, leaving behind it a loud echoing silence and a bright new gleaming world of yellow.

The men crouched in the backs of the trucks for what seemed a long time, caked with sand and unwilling to move, as if they could not believe that their ordeal was over. Slowly, very slowly, with arms dripping sand, outstretched like those of blind men, they felt for their sand-covered bodies.

Schirmer raised himself, sand dropping off his body in soft flurries. He took off his goggles and wiped his face. The entire area had changed. He licked his parched lips and stared at the transformed desert and what lay directly ahead, as if he were seeing a mirage.

Next to him White Lightning raised himself with a groan and began wiping the caked particles of sand from his face. Suddenly he also stopped and stared in the same direction as Schirmer. 'Holy mackerel,' he exclaimed, 'it's . . . it's an oasis!'

Schirmer nodded. 'Yes, it is . . . and look at that ruin beyond.' He indicated the stone pillars rising beyond the dusty palms and fringes of bushes. 'If I'm not mistaken, Major, they've been here a couple of years or more.'

'By God, sir, you're right!' White Lightning bounded to his feet, suddenly filled with tremendous enthusiasm. 'You know where we are, sir, don't you?' He didn't wait for a slower Colonel Schirmer to answer. Instead he yelled: 'One'll get you five, sir. But for my money, *we've found old Hannibal's elephant route* . . .!'

TWO

A little awed, the Headhunters clustered around the centre of the ancient oasis which glittered in the bright sunlight, the ground looking as if it were covered in snow. But the snow was salt, ankle-deep salt, through which trickled a trace of brackish water, flanked on both sides by stunted dusty palms and other shrubs.

'I think they call these things *foggara*,' Schirmer hesitantly explained to his staff. 'They're man-made. You see, the dunes are like a sponge which can absorb water in two ways. Either from above – dew or surface rain – or from below, due to the upward seepage from the water-bearing porous rocks underneath. So in ancient times they tunneled the *foggara* into the earth – sometimes for kilometres – in order to obtain a steady flow of water the whole year round. The Arabs have lost the art, so,' he puffed out his cheeks in the Gallic fashion, 'I can only conclude that this place was built by the Romans or their like.'

Schulze spat out a mouthful of brackish dark-green water which was flowing out of the tunnel to the right. 'Give me good old Munich suds any day,' he said scornfully. 'Tastes like camel piss to me!'

Schirmer grinned. 'Who knows, you big rogue. It might well be just that. After all, there might well be a camel taking a leak at the other end of the tunnel.'

Schulze hastily wiped the back of his big paw across his lips and made rasping, spitting sounds, almost as if he believed the CO, while the others laughed.

Schirmer strolled on, while his men started to unpack their trucks for the night, for he had ordered they would halt for the rest of the day; the sand storm had taken a lot out of the Headhunters. They needed the rest. Before them, half buried in the desert scrub, lay the ruins, a tumble of masonry surmounted by six or seven stone pillars, weathered by centuries of desert storms, but with tracery and patterns still visible here and there.

'Roman, I would think,' Schirmer said reflectively. 'The ruins look pretty much like the ones you see on the coast.'

'But why would the Romans built a settlement out here in the middle of nowhere? After all, it is barren desert,' Pansy Petersen objected.

'But it wasn't *then!*' Schirmer answered, pausing and shading his eyes to stare up at the pillars. 'There is a theory that the Sahara is constantly expanding outwards, but that it was once the bread-basket of the Ancient World, a fertile place that supplied most of the Middle East with its wheat. They say that the trade winds which brought the rain changed, and the Romans helped the desert to spread by chopping down the cedar trees along the littoral in order to obtain wood to build their naval ships.'

'The same sort of things the coastal Arabs did in '45 after the Italians had been kicked out,' White Lightning agreed. 'They say they chopped down over a million trees that the spaghetti-eaters had planted in order to show their hatred.'

'Typical Arab,' Schirmer said. 'They are the world's greatest haters. But in any case, back two thousand years or so ago, those sort of things changed the whole weather picture. The rains washed the earth from the fields and left barren rock behind. The barren rock couldn't support the population. The people left and you got the desert, inhabited by . . .' he shrugged and stared at the far distance '. . . God knows whom?' Suddenly he remembered the strange Arabs on the camels and their prisoner, who was still fighting to regain consciousness. Tod was working hard on him already, eager to start squeezing the information they needed out of his battered, skinny frame. 'All we know of them,' Schirmer continued, 'is that traditionally the ones who were left here in this damned waste of sand were men who lived by their own laws and customs, preying on the coastal settlements and caravans from time to time – a vicious, strange folk.'

Pansy Petersen stared beyond the ruins at the desert stretching to the horizon, shimmering now in the late afternoon heat, and shivered dramatically. 'Don't like it,' he said, 'definitely don't like it one bit.' For a fleeting moment his flamboyant homosexual manner vanished to be replaced by one of grim earnestness. 'Damnit, Colonel, what are we doing out here anyway? What in three devils' names has all this,' he threw a manicured hand at the scene all around them, 'got to do with us? We are Germans. Why should we go on fighting like this for a foreign power in this arsehole of the world, just because when we were young and foolish we belonged to a so-called criminal organization – the SS? Then we were regarded as patriots, the bravest of the brave. Now . . .' He stopped miserably, as if overwhelmed by the enormity of it all.

The others stared at the big colonel, whose bronzed, tough face was as sombre as that of Petersen. Slowly he nodded his cropped head, 'I agree, Petersen, old chap, I agree,' he said, running his fingers over the inscription at the base of the pillar, reading it with his fingertips. '*Titus Caius Germanicus centurio III° Legio Augusta: Why*, you ask?' He thought of other legionnaires like themselves who had once stood by this self same pillar twenty centuries before, dreaming the same dreams, perhaps, asking the same questions. What had they thought when they had been told that they had been betrayed at home in Rome, as he and his men had been betrayed in Bonn? Had they fought on against the barbarians here in the desert, while back in the homeland the spineless money-bags and politicians had given in to the evil that had swept in from the East, just as its successor, Russian communism, was doing? Or had they given in, broken camp and retreated to their bases on the coast, and from thence to Rome itself? 'Perhaps Petersen,' he stumbled to find the right words,

'we are still the only patriots, the bravest of the brave, the
last defenders of a kind of civilization against the forces of
evil, the new barbarians – and we are defending it out here
just as much . . .'

'*Sir, sir!*' an excited, urgent voice cut into his clumsy
attempt to explain his own motives, 'he's one of us . . . *one
of us!*'

The officers turned round as one, startled. It was Spider
Arse, running in that strange lopsided gait of his, dragging
the leg that had nearly been severed at Stalingrad over
twelve years before behind him in the sand, his face red
and streaming with sweat.

'Where's the fire, Sergeant?' Schirmer called. 'What
gives?'

Spider Arse stumbled to a halt and threw his CO a shaky
salute, his skinny chest heaving with the effort of so much
running in that heat. 'It's Tod, sir . . . he told me to tell
you . . . The prisoner has come to and has started to sing,'
he swallowed hard and fought to control his breathing, his
eyes sparkling with excitement. 'And he's one of us!' he
burst out in a final flourish of words.

'One of us?' Schirmer barked. 'What the devil do you
mean – one of us?'

'He's German, sir. He ain't a slopehead after all . . .
German!'

'Look at this, sir,' Tod said excitedly, rolling back the
man's gown as he lay there, moaning weakly under the
shade of the awning.

The arm was as brown as any Arab's to the elbow, but
after that it became pure white. The dying man was no
Arab, that was certain. But there was more to come.
Brutally, the little ex-Gestapo torturer turned the upper
arm to one side and proudly stepped back to let Schirmer
see what he had discovered there.

The big colonel gasped with surprise and Tod smirked
with pleasure as Schirmer stared down at the fading

numerals tattooed there in black. 'The blood group,' he said a little weakly. 'He's one of us . . . *he's SS!*'[1] He looked rather wildly from the prisoner, whose nose had already acquired the pinched look of someone soon to die, to a happily smirking Tod, his eyes gleaming behind his nickel-framed schoolmaster's spectacles. 'But how . . . what?' he stuttered and then, swallowing hard, added, 'a deserter from the Legion perhaps?'

Tod shook his head. 'No, sir,' he announced pompously. 'He only left Germany three months ago. He told me so himself – after a – er – little persuasion.'

Schirmer overcame his revulsion at the thought of Tod torturing a dying man and said, 'But in God's name, what is he doing here – in the middle of nowhere, man?'

'Of course, I haven't got all the details yet, sir.' He flung an anxious glance at the man lying in the sand, his chest heaving as if he was fighting for breath. 'But he was definitely watching us with the other two who got away.'

'*Watching us!*' Schirmer exploded. 'But what would a German be doing watching us out here . . . and how did he know that we were heading this way?' He tried to control his rising fury and failed. 'For God's sake, man, don't play shitting cat-and-mouse with me. Cough it up!'

Tod swallowed hard, suddenly afraid. 'It was the French colonel . . . Colonel de Gray, sir, he's working for them. He put this man and the others on our tracks.'

Schirmer breathed out hard. 'Schulze, you've always got some fire-water hidden away somewhere or other. For God's sake, have mercy on a sorely-tried man and give me a swift slug before I lose my reason!'

Schulze handed over his second canteen. As Schirmer had suspected, it was not filled with water as regulations prescribed. The fiery hot liquid which ran down his throat was native date arak. He breathed out gratefully and handed back the canteen. 'Now, Tod,' he continued, in

[1] In order to facilitate quick treatment of their wounded, troopers of the wartime SS had their blood group marked thus.

control of himself once again. 'Colonel de Gray, you allege, is a traitor, working for – I presume – the FLN?'

'Exactly, sir.'

'This man and the others who escaped were also members of the FLN, at least the Arabs were, and they were told of our route by de Gray?'

'Yes sir.' The young ex-SS man at Tod's feet moaned suddenly, his thin, ashen face contorted with agony. Tod frowned. The man hadn't long to live and the colonel was wasting time.

'But why? Was there any particular reason for them to watch us? Surely de Gray would, if what you say is true, have told them about our objective – the Red Oasis, if it exists?'

'Probably, sir,' Tod answered hurriedly, as the prisoner started to stir with the restlessness that precedes death in the violently injured. 'But apparently it wasn't our attempt to find the Red Oasis that concerned them. In fact, the prisoner had never even heard of the place. I asked him specifically, my very first question, in fact.' He beamed up at Schirmer as if he expected praise for his foresight.

'Oh, for God's sake, don't be so damned full of yourself!' Schirmer snapped in irritation. He bent on one knee next to the dying man, wiping away the thick glistening beads of sweat from his forehead and smoothing back the lock of damp, blond hair. Suddenly he visualized the many times he had knelt thus at the side of similar blond youths from the *Leibstandarte, Hitlerjugend, Wotan* and all the rest of the elite SS divisions during the war, comforting them before they commenced their last journey. The prisoner was no different: he had been one of them. He still was. 'So, why did the poor shit have to buy it in this God-forsaken place at the hands of his own people, Tod?' he rasped, looking up at the torturer.

'Because, sir, it was thought that we might get in their way.' He saw the look on Schirmer's face and continued hurriedly before there were any more angry outbursts. 'You see, sir, one day's march from here, they are going to make an air-drop or something of that kind. He was already beginning to fade when I got to that stage . . . an air-drop of weapons for the desert Arabs. Now . . .'

'Shut up!' Schirmer cut him short, concentrating on the unknown youth, who had once been one of them.

A faint rasping sound was coming from deep, deep within him and his eyes had flickered open. Schirmer bent low to attempt to make them out, while the youth's hand sought and found his. He returned the pressure, knowing it would be a matter of seconds now. 'What is it, son?' he whispered, face close to the youth's, which glistened now, as if covered with hot grease. 'It's going to be all right. Don't worry, we're going to get you to an MO soon. The bone-menders'll patch you up, I'll see to that . . .' He heard himself saying the same old clichés of comfort that he had used so many times before. 'Don't you worry about a thing . . .'

'Egypt . . . the planes are coming from Egypt,' the youth whispered, his eye-lids flickering wildly now, as he fought death to the very last. 'Refuel and turn-about . . . Double quick time . . .' Surprisingly the dying youth grinned. '*Jawohl, Sturmbannfuhrer,*' he croaked in a mockery of the crisp military style of the SS, *'wird's gemacht. Die Weiber bringen wir heute . . .'*[1]

Suddenly his whole body arched like a taut bow string. His fingers dug hard into Schirmer's palm. A horrible rattling sound shook his skinny frame, while his lips drew back to expose teeth set in the final grimace of death.

'Water!' Schirmer snapped urgently.

Too late. The youth's head fell to one side. The light went out of his eyes. Next moment his body sagged back to the hot sand, a sudden trickle of black blood seeping out of the left side of his mouth, set and gaping in the last yellow mask.

For a while no one moved under the awning. Outside there was no sound save the faint whisper of the breeze in the dusty palm leaves and the muted lazy sounds exhausted

[1] 'We'll bring in the dames this . . .'

men make as they prepare for sleep. Slowly, Schirmer reached up and pulled down the dead man's eyelids with that old practised movement that he hated. He rose ponderously and touched his hand to his camouflage cap in salute. 'He *was* one of us,' he said, without looking at the others who had stumbled to their feet automatically. 'Search him for documents, ID etc,' he ordered, his voice devoid of any emotion save weariness, 'then bury him so that the jackals can't get at him.' He walked outside, blinking abruptly in the hard oblique rays of the setting sun. Almost as an afterthought, he called over his shoulder, 'All officers and senior noncoms report to me for a conference in one hour's time.' Then he stamped off towards the ruins, his broad shoulders bent, as if in defeat.

Numbly they stared after him.

THREE

Now it was nearly dawn. Still the desert was cool, though to the east the dull white of the pre-dawn sky was tinged a faint pink, indicating another bakingly hot day to come. Most of the Headhunters were prepared for it, though. During the night, in spite of being worn out after the previous day's long motor march, they had dug pits for themselves into the sand, covering them with camel scrub which was plentiful in the area of the DZ.[1] Thereafter they had turned their attention to the vehicles, covering them with the same scrub and rolling boulders and heavy stones about them to break up their shape, so that any casual airborne observer would take them for a series of large boulders.

Some still slept after the exertions of the night, but most were already awake, chewing dry ration crackers and dates, or taking cautious sips at their water (for Schirmer had ordered it to be strictly rationed; there would be no moving out into the open to the trucks to fetch fresh supplies this particular day), their eyes constantly flicking to the east from which the planes must come.

'It all fits in now, gentlemen,' Schirmer said softly, staring around at the unshaven faces of Schulze, White Lightning and Petersen who shared the command post with him. 'Moscow is using communist East Germany as the supplier of arms to the rebels – hence the up-dated Schmeissers. We Germans have better contacts with Egypt than they do, after all, Nasser did work for the German

[1] Dropping zone.

Abwehr[1] against the British during the war. So at the Kremlin's command, supplies of weapons, ammo etc. are flown from East Berlin to Egypt and from there to here. Naturally, people like that arch-traitor de Gray would become aware of such flights in due course – he is closest to the DZs – and so he had to be bought off. Money, pretty boys,' he shrugged carelessly.

'Oh, la, la,' Petersen simpered, in spite of his cramped position. 'I like pretty boys, too!'

Schirmer smiled wearily. 'I'll buy you a whole cageful of them, Petersen, when we get back to Algiers.'

If a little voice at the back of White Lightning's head added, but he did not say the thought aloud. Instead he said, 'Well, if everything that dead kid back there said is true and the East Germans are going to be running in a supply of arms to the rebels today, *which* rebels are they intended for?'

'I have given a lot of thought to that question, Major, and my guess is that they can only be meant for the Caid's people. I can't see the soft sisters of the city FLN coming out so far into the desert to receive them. Besides, there is enough clandestine boat traffic along the coast which could supply them with what they need.'

'So that means, sir, that there is a Red Oasis somewhere out there after all?' Schulze said, wishing he dare reach for his second canteen with the arak in it and have a good swig before the day's action started, but knowing he daren't, not in the CO's presence.

Schirmer nodded.

'And that's where there's got to be a reception committee then – to pick up the weapons?' Petersen added quickly.

'Yes,' Schirmer agreed and pushed his little cap to the back of his head, 'and that brings us to our major problem.'

'What's that, sir?' White Lightning asked, as outside the sky to the east began to flush its first dramatic blood-red of the new day.

[1] As young Egyptian Army officers, Nasser and Sadat worked with German Intelligence in an attempt to overthrow the British in WWII.

'What our course of action is to be? Do we nobble them before the planes arrive? Tod, I am confident, can get the location out of them – the location of the Red Oasis, that is – or do we wait till after the drop? You see, unless the pilots receive some special sort of signal from the ground, they may not drop their weapons. Not only that, they may also be in a position to warn the tribesmen at the Red Oasis about what's going on. Then, although we capture the weapons, the leaders of the revolt will survive to fight another day.'

For a while they pondered the problem, as the sky began to lighten rapidly and the murderous heat started to increase by the second. Finally White Lightning broke the silence saying, 'Well, as you know, sir, in airborne ops anything can go wrong and usually does. Remember some of the Sbafus we experienced in Vietnam and, brother, I could tell you some of the lulu-lulus we had in Europe in the Old War with the Screaming Eagles![1] so most transport pilots on these ops are only too glad to make out any kind of signal, drop their bundles and beat it back home.'

'So?' Schirmer queried, staring at the American's hairless, gauntly handsome face. He suddenly realized White Lightning still missed his old outfit, although its commanding general had once sentenced him to death; his weary, red-rimmed eyes had lit up at the very mention of the 101st Airborne.

'So, sir, I say, nobble the slopeheads first. Even if we can't get the exact signal correct – we can assume that even under, er, pressure, from Tod they might trick us – the pilots up there will conclude that the slopeheads got it wrong and drop their goodies. Besides, they'll take the slopeheads for the ignorant bastards that they are.'

Schirmer pursed his lips and considered for a few moments. White Lightning, he told himself, was right. It was better for him to be in charge of the DZ, that way nothing on the ground was left to chance. With a bit of

[1] Nickname for the US 101st Airborne Division.

luck the pilots of the weapon carriers would react the way the American had suggested. 'I should imagine you're right, Major,' he said after a moment. 'Besides, the pilots won't suspect that there is anyone else out here in this God-forsaken desert, will they?'

The others nodded their agreement, all save Schulze, who suddenly looked glum. Schirmer glanced at him. 'Well, you big rogue, where's the fire? Are you worried about that rotgut firewater you've got strapped to the back of your big Hamburg arse?'

'No, sir,' Schulze answered unhappily. 'It isn't that at all.'

'Well, piss or get off the pot, speak out, man!' Schirmer snapped, face set in a good-humoured grin, now all the basic details of the ambush had been worked out to his satisfaction.

'Well, sir,' Schulze said slowly, 'I thought I heard that poor stiff back there say something just before he croaked which doesn't quite fit in with what we've planned.'

All eyes turned in his direction, as from outside there came the unmistakable dry metallic sound of a rifle bolt being drawn back softly, followed a second later by a stirring all along the series of camouflage pits.

Schirmer registered the sounds with a quick stirring of his blood as the adrenalin began to pump. 'Come on, Schulze, you're not usually so slow at sounding off, you big rogue. What do you think you heard?'

'I thought he said something about re-fuelling and a quick turn-about,' Schulze answered miserably, lowering his gaze to the sand, as if he could not face looking his CO in the eye.

'So, we have to change our plans a little, if that is the case,' Schirmer snapped. Now there was definitely activity taking place outside. Perhaps the slopehead reception party was coming. Time was running out; they hadn't much more to waste.

'But you don't see, sir!'

'What don't I see?' Schirmer asked, strapping on his

pistol belt hastily, as the excited chatter outside grew in volume.

'If they're coming from East Germany, they'll be German – they might even be from the SS like ourselves.' Schulze gulped painfully, head twisted to one side, as if he were having great difficulty in getting the words out, 'And if they land, sir, we'll have to . . . to engage them.' The rest came out in a quick rush. *'Sir, we'll have to fight our own people!'*

Sergeant-Major Schulze crouched behind the little parapet made of rocks and camel scrub, feeling the sun beat down on his back scorchingly, although it was only eight o'clock in the morning, the sweat dripping from his furrowed brow in a steady stream. Immediate ahead of him, the camel train advanced ever deeper into the trap, the faint cries of the drivers already quite clearly audible in the still, hot air. They obviously suspected nothing. Cautiously, Schulze wiped his brow for the umpteenth time and thought longingly of Algiers and the sea. He'd buy himself a couple of whores when they got back, not the usual shapeless slopeheads, but a couple of high-priced French whores – even if he had to steal the battalion funds to do it. Then he'd check in at one of the de luxe hotels along the beach where the breeze came in fresh and cool straight from the sea, order two – no, three cases of champus – and lock the door for forty-eight hours. His big red face was suddenly wreathed in a smiles at the prospect. By the great whore of Buxtehude, where the gash hangs from the trees, that would be a time and a half! Forty-eight hours with two *grandes horizontales*, as the Frogs called them, as much chilled champus as he could drink, all tucked in a big double bed with a mattress as soft as mother's tit! He licked his parched lips. *Then*, he could die happy.

'Schulze!' Spider Arse's voice cut into his sexual reveries.

'What is it?' he hissed angrily. 'You stupid horned-ox,

I was just getting the knickers off'n a high-priced Frog hoor and you interrupt me. Ain't you got no heart?'

'*The CO*'ll have your knickers off yer in double-quick time,' Spider Arse sneered, 'if you don't get yer digit out of the orifice! They're almost there. Time for the signal.'

Schulze forgot the high-titted whores with their shaven loins and flashed a look ahead. The last camel, laden heavily with what he thought were gasoline cans, had passed their marker, a large white boulder. Now they were well and truly within the hollow three-sided square formed by the hidden Headhunters. He swallowed hard. Veteran that he was, he still felt apprehension at this moment: the moment of blood, when the killing has to start once again. For he knew, like all the seasoned 'Old Heads' did, that one day he would not survive; but become one of the huddled, abandoned bundles on the battlefield which marked yet another life snuffed out in the snap of a finger and thumb. He raised his pistol.

'Jesus H,' Spider Arse hissed, 'what are you waiting for – a shitting written invitation? Fire!'

Schulze hesitated no longer. He pressed the trigger of the big barrelled pistol. A soft crack. A hiss. A thin streak of black smoke as the cartridge soared high into the brilliant blue sky. One of the camels shied. A group of Arabs turned and stared in bewildered alarm. Someone cried something in guttural desert Arabic. The signal flare exploded with a muted crack. It hung there a brilliant, incandescent white directly above the camel train, turning the brown upturned faces an eerie glowing hue, as they cried out to one another in wonder and sudden rage.

Suddenly the camels broke to left and right. Frightening screams of hoarse, exultant, vindictive rage rose on all sides, as the tribesmen realized what had happened and urged their ungainly, heavily-laden beasts forward.

Schulze's blood turned to ice. They were racing straight for him and Spider Arse in their lonely outpost. Why had no shit fired yet? *They were coming straight at him!*

At his side Spider Arse yelled, '*Los*, slopeheads . . . come *to Daddy!* . . . Come and take a bit of steel titty!' He pressed the trigger of his grease gun. The weapon jerked like a live thing at his side. Veteran that he was, he swayed from side to side, spraying lead in a forty-five degree arc. An Arab racing full-tilt on his camel screamed as his arms flailed the air. Next instant he had slapped into the desert, the crazy beast racing on riderless. Another camel driver took a full burst in the face. It looked as if someone had thrown a handful of red jam at it. He fell, screaming, on the neck of his animal in a welter of flying red. Suddenly Schulze awoke from his paralysis. The main body of the Arabs, bent low over the long, outstretched necks of their racing beasts, their ungainly legs flying across the desert at a tremendous rate, had swerved to the left. Instinctively they had realized they had to break out to one of the flanks if they were to escape the tremendous fire coming from the front and two sides. Now, some fifty or sixty of them were hurtling towards the outpost postions held by Schulze and a handful of the Headhunters. If they didn't hold, they'd be through and into the safety of the desert beyond.

Schulze sprang out from behind his cover, ignoring the slugs cutting through the air as the rest of the Headhunters turned their fire on the breakout site. 'The Captain's got a hole in his arse,' he cried joyfully, his initial fear forgotten now in that wild bloodlust of battle, carried away by the crazy exuberance of danger and imminent death. '*UP IT, COMRADES!*'

Infected by the NCO's mad enthusiasm, the other Headhunters did the same. Crouched like western gunslingers in some final shoot-out, they stood there in line, machine-pistols spitting fire, throwing a solid wall of bullets directly in the path of the racing camels. The ugly beasts went down on all sides, rearing up in their death agonies, thrashing their spindly legs, sinking to their haunches, brown shaggy sides patched with scarlet, what looked like red buttonholes stitched the length of their heaving flanks, whimpering, bellowing with unbearable agony.

Like skilled acrobats, their riders vaulted over their heads and came on screeching with rage, weapons at the ready. Too late, they realized their danger as the first Arab stumbled on the deadly trip-wire planted so cunningly in the loose sand. He tried to get up – and away. Too late. Yellow light flashed blindingly. All along the length of Schulze's positions, vicious little spurts of flame erupted. The Headhunters raised their arms in front of their faces and, ducking, half-turned. They knew what was to come. The desert shook like a live thing. The Arabs desperately tried to keep their balance, wailing in abject fear. With a crazy roar, the minefield, grenades interlinked by fuse-wire, erupted. The surviving Arabs and their beasts went sailing through the air, a whirling mass of severed limbs and mangled bodies, human and animal. A gasoline container exploded in a vicious ball of scarlet flame. Oily fire streamed down onto the camel bearing it. It ran round in circles, bleating for mercy. Next instant the whole animal disintegrated. Schulze ducked hastily as a severed head came flying his way.

'Holy strawsack,' Spider Arse breathed in awe, as the bloody head slammed into the sand just behind them, 'what'll they throw shitting next?'

He'd hardly spoken when the shattered headless body of one of the riders dropped out of the sky at his feet, a meaty mess of twisted, gory flesh and bones, from which the blood jetted in a thick scarlet stream like the juice of a rich ripe fig.

'God in Heaven . . . Why do they keep sending them in pieces?' he cried in mock exasperation.

But Schulze was in no mood for Spider Arse's perverted battle-ground humour. 'Knock it off, smart-ass!' he snapped, suddenly sickened by the slaughter, as the survivors of the ambush began to slide from their beasts and, like sleep-walkers, hands raised nervously, started to walk to Colonel Schirmer's positions to surrender. 'All right . . . all right,' he called above the dying snap-and-crackle of small-arms fire, 'cease fire . . . Come on, get the shitting wax out of yer spoons – *ceasefire!*'

He waited until it was safe and the last trigger-happy young Headhunter had lowered his smoking grease gun, then he strode forward and routinely started to shoot the surviving camels as they writhed in the red, scuffed sand in their death throes. 'Pick up the slopeheads,' he called over his shoulder, not looking up from his self-imposed task. Camels were ugly creatures, but he couldn't watch dumb animals suffer like this. 'Start getting the rest of this stuff under cover – and then yourselves. We don't want the flyboys to suspect anything when they come.' He pointed to an Arab, whose leg had been severed at the knee and now sat in a pool of his own blood, holding his skinny claw to his main artery and staring up at the Headhunters advancing towards him with undisguised hatred. 'Pick that one up – and be careful that he ain't got a carving knife hidden up his nightshirt – and take him over to that shit Tod so he can put the squeeze on him. He's just the kind of jailbait Gestapo Tod loves . . .'

Suddenly Schulze felt the energy drain out of him, as if someone had just opened a tap. His legs abruptly became like jelly. He had to sit down. He *did* sit down in the middle of the dead, sprawled out in the careless, abandoned postures of men killed in battle, and the awkward ugly corpses of the camels upon which the greedy blue flies had already begun to settle in humming, excited clouds.

He pushed his kepi back from his sweat-damp forehead and looked weakly at his big paws. They were trembling like he had never seen them tremble before, even after a week of hard drinking. What was the matter with him? He had been killing like this for nearly fifteen years now, ever since he had joined Wotan back in 1939 as a nineteen-year-old. He had killed Tommies, Belgies, Frogs, spaghetti-eaters, Greeks, Amis, Niggers, Chinks, Gooks, slopeheads, men and women of every goddam colour under the sun. Why should this minor skirmish in the middle of nowhere upset him? What was wrong? *What?*

Abruptly he had it with the startling clarity of a premonition. He had survived this skirmish and he would soldier on a little while longer. But he would never leave the desert now – he knew that. He thought of Hamburg and the waterfront, the bars and brothels of the Reeperbahn and the little sailors' drinking dens down by the church in St Pauli, the smart little broads and the petty crooks with whom he had grown up, and croaked hoarsely, 'I'll never see them again.'

Slowly, a solitary tear began to trickle down his tough, leathery face. For the first time in his whole life since that day when he was twelve and he had been kicked out of his local *Volksschule* for having attempted to put his hand up the skirt of Fraulein Handke, Sergeant-Major Schulze, holder of the Knight's Cross, German Cross in Gold, all classes of the Iron Cross, *Medaille Militaire, Croix de Guerre avec Palme*, sat there in the sand and sobbed like a little boy . . .

FOUR

'Flight Commander, take over,' Major Trautgott Timmermann snapped, leaning away from the controls with a sigh of relief, feeling his leather jacket stick to his back with the sweat. He had been flying the old Dakota belonging to the Egyptian Air Force ever since they had refuelled at Benghazi; he needed a rest before the landing. Let Flight Commander Sanders take over for a while.

'*Jawohl, Herr Major*,' Sanders snapped happily, as if he were back on the parade ground in Potsdam, and took over the controls.

Timmermann smiled cynically and looked at Sanders' keen, handsome young face out of the corner of his eye. The kid was a Prussian to his fingertips though, of course, thanks to the victors, Prussia had not existed since 1945. He had even shaved in the hour they had spent at Benghazi, although water had been rationed there as if it were good Berlin beer. He tried to make himself comfortable in the sticky leather seat and lit a cigarette, although it was forbidden; but then everything was forbidden in the new Socialist Workers' and Farmers' Paradise east of the River Elbe. Hell, he told himself, taking a deep contented drag of the American cigarette, bought on the black market in Cairo, the new commie masters were stricter than the blacks[1] had been in the good old days.

He turned slowly and stared back at the confused but orderly mess of machine-guns, hung with gleaming yellow cartridge belts, oxygen bottles, sanitary buckets and all the rest of their gear, with the two British-built Horsa gliders

[1] Nickname for the SS.

95

fifty metres or so behind the tug. They were keeping their position nicely, he told himself, looking at them with a practised eye. Even the heat thermals rising from the shimmering desert far below didn't bother the pilots. But then they shouldn't. They were the cream of the new East German 'People's Army' glider pilots, all veterans of the SS Parachute Corps, to which he had once belonged himself. 'Yer,' a cynical little voice at the back of his sleek blond head sneered, 'who else but you shits would fly a crazy mission like this – the villains of the armed SS?'

Timmermann took another lazy drag at his cigarette, the blue smoke curling up and making him wrinkle up his bright bold eyes. Who indeed? But what other alternative had they had? Now, or then, back in 1948, when the *Vopos*[1] and the men from Mielke's *SSD*[2] had come for him in the middle of the night at the farmhouse where he had been working as a farm-labourer ever since he had taken a 'dive' after the defeat of 1945. They had knocked him about a bit – a couple of his excellent white teeth had gone in the process – but he had expected that. He had *not* expected what they had offered him. It had been either twenty-five years hard labour for war crimes, to be served in the Gulag, courtesy of their Russian 'brothers'; or recruitment to the new clandestine wing of the embryo 'People's Air Force', Special Duties Section. He had suddenly been overcome, as he had explained to the cautious-eyed, hard-faced men of the SSD, by 'socialist ardour'. He had 'volunteered' there and then; along with another eight hundred former SS men who had been trained as pilots, glider pilots and parachutists during the war. Since then they had run a dozen crazy missions like this one: running weapons into Albanian over the heads of the 'Jugs', who were no longer 'socialist brothers' since Tito had broken with Moscow; supplying the slopeheads with know-how in their fight against the Yids; parachuting agents into Wales to the nationalists; one damned op after

[1] People's Police.
[2] Intelligence Service.

another, and every time someone had bought it and never returned. 'Still, there are plenty more of you, aren't there?' General Hoffmann, their commander-in-chief, had commented airily, after presenting him with a bit of red tin, which was some new socialist decoration (he had pinned it up in the officers' thunderbox). 'We've got cages of tame SS men, only too willing to devote their lives to socialism – *for the price of a litre of suds–and a bit of slit!*' Timmermann grinned at the memory. Hoffmann was as cynical as he was himself.

Suddenly he frowned. He had never been on such a crazy mission as this one. Two thousand kilometres across the desert, most of it uncharted, to make an unmarked DZ. There to cast off the two gliders laden with weapons and the poor fools of instructors who had 'volunteered' (their families were being held as hostages at SSD Headquarters to ensure they 'volunteered') and then to land and re-fuel for the long haul home. God, there were so many imponderables! What if they missed the DZ? Or if the slopeheads didn't turn up? What were they going to use for gas for the long haul back to Benghazi – the piss-buckets at the back of this creaking old tub that the Amis must have flogged to the Gippos back in 1942? Abruptly Major Trautgott Timmermann, formerly of the *Waffen SS*, who had been personally decorated three times by the Fuhrer for bravery at the Wolf's Lair, mopped his brow. He told himself that if he pursued this line of thought any longer, he'd be creaming his skivvies like some young greenhorn, still wet behind the spoons, going into combat for the very first time.

'How we going, Flight Commander?' he asked swiftly, taking malicious delight in using young Sanders' official title.

'*Alles in Butter, Herr Major*,' Sanders answered proudly, sitting bolt upright in his seat, as if he were behind the controls of some brand new MIG jet instead of this beaten-up old kite, tied together with string and spit.

Timmermann grinned in spite of his growing sense of

apprehension. Sanders had not been corrupted like the rest of them. He enjoyed the missions, but then he was young, still wet behind the spoons. He had only been sixteen when the Ivans had put him behind Swedish curtains back in 1945. He had not experienced the full bitterness of the defeat after all those years of bloodshed and desperate self-sacrifice, as had the older members of Hitler's vaunted Black Guards.

Sanders started to bring the old crate down. Timmermann did not need to check the altimeter to know that. He could feel it as the temperature began to rise. He glanced out of the cockpit. What a hell-hole, he told himself, grimly, a real devil's country! How could one find one's way down there? The only thing you could do would be to orientate yourself on any object that stuck out of the glowing sea of sand, a camel's skeleton, a pile of stones, a rusty petrol can – things like that, he supposed.

Sanders abruptly thrust up his sunglasses and craned his neck forward. Timmermann forgot his strange sense of apprehension. 'See anything?' he rasped.

'Think so,' Sanders, who had very keen eyesight, answered. 'To port, among that patch of boulders or whatever they are.'

Timmermann reached for the binoculars hanging from the ceiling and focused them hurriedly.

Dark shapes slid into the gleaming circles of calibrated glass, and they were waving furiously, some of them even jumping up and down in their excitement, robes flapping. 'Typical niggers,' he commented, lowering the glasses, and adding for Sanders' benefit, for he half-suspected that Sanders had begun to fall for the communist line, 'not that I'm racially prejudiced. Just can't stand niggers at the bar!'

Sanders frowned and looked worried.

Timmermann gently nudged him in the ribs. 'Don't worry, old friend,' he said, for he liked the boy really, 'there are no nasty little men with big boots from the Ministry of State Security listening. Here you're among friends. We can say what we like . . . I think the Führer was right, give 'em some nuts and send them back up the trees.'

Sanders gasped. '*Herr Major!*'

'*Herr Major*, my arse, let's concentrate on getting rid of our load and landing this heap of shit,' Timmermann cut in crudely. He eyed the DZ with a practised eye, as Sanders came lower and lower, the gliders now riding slightly above them, their pilots obviously working hard to avoid crashing into one another in the turbulence that came from the Dakota and the ground thermals. It looked fairly clear with firm sand, the only obstacle the many boulders to port which Sanders had spotted. He made his decision. 'You handle the controls, Sanders, I'll take care of the gliders. We'll release them first, the poor shits, see what kind of a landing they make. Then we come in.' He grinned in that crooked, cynical manner of his. 'If they take the purple shaft up the arse, then we'll know what to avoid, won't we?'

Sanders said nothing, but Timmermann could see the look of disapproval on his handsome young face. 'Hard shit,' he told himself. 'You'll learn, my boy, before you're finished, you'll learn. In this world, it's dog eat dog.' Then he forgot Sanders and concentrated on the task before him, as the pilot brought the Dakota round in a slow wide circle, while below the Arabs waved furiously. 'Coconut One, do you read me?' He pressed this throat mike and from the first tug, the boozy voice of ex-*Sturmbannfuhrer* Streich, formerly of the *Leibstandarte*, came crackling over the radio.

'I read you . . . I read . . . What's the deal?'

'You go in first on the second turn. Watch those boulders – they could bring back your migraine. It is that time of the month for you, isn't it?'

'Kiss my arse, *Herr Major*,' Streich answered. 'I was flying these crates while you were still filling yer triangular drawers.'

Timmermann smiled and pressed this throat mike again. 'Coconut Two . . . you're going in on the third turn after Streich. All right?'

The pilot of Coconut Two who, with the rest of the instructors, had 'volunteered' to stay in the desert said, 'Sure, what could be wrong? While you're back there in Berlin, slipping a link into all those brave Young Pioneers[1] and knocking back suds till they come out of yer ears, I'll be toasting myself in the desert with a lot of friendly niggers – with not a care in the shitting world. Of course, everything is shitting all right! Over and out.'

Timmermann shook his head fondly. He'd miss Storch in the mess and their regular forty-eight hour benders at the weekend. Storch was a great sauce-hound, one of the best.

'*Gut*, Sanders,' he commanded, very professional now, pressing the red warning light for the first glider. 'You can cast off Coconut One – *now!*'

Sanders flicked the toggle and immediately grabbed the controls with both hands, automatically revving the port engine as the Dakota shuddered, suddenly released from the burden of the first glider.

Timmermann flashed a look to the side. Streich had reacted perfectly. To counteract the moment of release, he had brought the big glider's nose up. Now it seemed to hover there in mid-air like a great green hawk and Timmermann could visualize Streich fighting the controls, waiting until it was out of range of the Dakota's prop wash before he began his final descent. Sanders began to bring the American transport round for a second turn. Timmermann pressed the red warning button which alerted the pilot of the second glider. Streich was now levelling out. In a moment he would begin his dive.

Timmerman flashed a last look below. The Arabs were still waving, as if they were expecting Father Christmas complete with sledge and goodies to descend upon them at any moment. He sniffed. 'You can cast off Coconut Two . . . *now!*'

Sanders hit the release. The Dakota jerked. It sailed up a good fifty metres before Sanders caught it and then they

[1] Communist Youth Organization in East Germany.

were completing their circle. Behind them, the two gliders started to go in, separated from each other by a good two hundred metres. Timmermann nodded his approval. Everything seemed to be going perfectly. Now the only problem was the landing. He leaned forward intently, while at his side Sanders turned and grinned at him triumphantly.

Timmermann shrugged, suddenly irritated by such youthful innocence. 'I'll see they award you another piece of that cheap red enamel for this one,' he snapped. 'Outstanding devotion – and all that crap!'

Sanders flushed hotly and quickly turned his attention back to the controls.

Schirmer slowly lowered his binoculars. The first glider was coming in to land. He knew the technique. The pilot would level out at about a hundred metres from the deck, then lift the plane's nose to act as a brake, trying to get his landing speed down to less than a hundred kilometres an hour and come in. He frowned and said a little prayer that the frail craft of wood and canvas would contain only Egyptians. At his side, Schulze stared at him intently. Schirmer knew why, but he ignored the look.

'What do you think then, sir?' White Lightning asked, lowering his own glasses. He had been staring at the old Dakota, 'the work-horse of the sky', as they had called the plane back in the good old days with the Screaming Eagles. 'About the tug up there, sir? Is it going to land once the gliders are down?'

'Perhaps not. Perhaps that poor stiff got it wrong? Perhaps Tod didn't get it right?'

'But the camels *were* carrying fuel, sir,' White Lightning objected. 'And you don't need fuel for gliders,' he added significantly.

Schirmer frowned. 'You're right, of course, you don't need gasoline for gliders.' He swung round urgently to a waiting Petersen. 'Pansy,' he snapped, 'get your best marksmen on the job. Whatever happens, don't let that plane get away.'

Petersen smiled. He liked a challenge. 'Regard it as done. Those machine-gunners of mine could part yer hair at two hundred metres.' He dashed away to carry out the order.

Now the lead glider was only two hundred metres from the ground, skimming in at an incredibly steep angle, while on the DZ, Headhunters dressed in the robes taken from dead tribesmen were waving furiously, as if their very lives depended upon it, their faces red and glistening with sweat.

'Schulze, your men in position?'

The big noncom swallowed hard. 'But sir, what if they are . . .'

'I asked you a question, Sarnt-Major!' Schirmer cut into Schulze's objection brutally. 'What's your answer?'

'They're in position, sir,' Schulze answered miserably.

'Good, remember then that both gliders have to be down before you start anything.'

'Perhaps we could ask them to surrender?'

Schirmer shook his head. 'No,' he rasped, 'it has to be done swiftly, with no hesitation . . . like a surgeon amputating a gangrenous limb that could infect the whole body if it weren't taken off at once. Understand, Schulze?'

'I understand sir,' Schulze said and turned away without another word, his big shoulders bent.

'Sir!' It was White Lightning.

'Yes?'

'Here comes the first one. Look, sir!' White Lightning pointed to the DZ, where the 'Arabs' were scattering wildly now to get out of the way of the big glider hurtling towards them. 'They're landing!'

Schirmer flashed a look at Schulze's gunners. They were in position, concealed behind the boulders. From there his gaze flew to the tug. The Dakota was still droning round in lazy circles in the brilliant blue sky, but the plane did seem lower than it had a few moments earlier. Soon it would attempt to land and run into the same trap they had set for the gliders. 'Get ready!' he barked above the hiss of the wind underneath the great green wings of the glider, which was almost down now, every detail of its canvas fuselage visible, even to the painted-out insignia of the Egyptian Air Force.

'*She's down!*' someone cried excitedly, as two thousand pounds of men and material hit the desert with a hellish thwack. The glider was immediately submerged in a huge, whirling cloud of yellow sand, its skids screeching ear-splittingly as they attempted to brake the plane, the wire wrapped around them to speed up the braking process snapping like twine.

'Here comes number two now!' White Lightning cried as the first glider hurtled across the desert at an impossible speed, trailing a tremendous wake behind it, the pilot fighting desperately to brake the plane before it smashed into the litter of boulders straight ahead.

Schirmer bit his bottom lip. Now there was only the plane. He shaded his eyes and threw a look upwards. It was definitely coming down. He could see that the pilot had lowered the flaps and its speed had dropped. To his right, Petersen's gunners were already following its course intently with their light machine-guns, just in case.

The second glider came swishing down. It hit the desert with the grinding scream of air brakes and protesting wooden fuselage. It slewed to the right and the pilot caught it just in time. It straightened up and bounced ten metres into the air. A skid came off and fluttered to the sand. A second later it shuddered to a grinding, rending halt. Swaying and shuddering, one wing splintered as it hit a boulder, it staggered to a stop in a thick, choking cloud of dust. For a moment no one moved outside or inside the two gliders. There was no sound save the tense breathing of the ambushers and the steady drone of the Dakota. Shakily, the door of the first glider was pushed open.

Schirmer hesitated no longer. He raised his right arm and let it drop with a great '*FEUER!*'

What happened next was not war, but murder – the pitiless massacre of the defenceless figures crowded in the doorway in their overlong shorts and bright new khaki uniforms. Instead of being greeted by shouts of welcome from the natives they had come to help 'liberate' themselves, they were met by a solid wall of fire.

Uncomprehending, stunned and confused by the terrible thing that was happening to them, they simply stood there and allowed themselves to be slaughtered like dumb animals, spinning and collapsing, as the bullets thwacked into their defenceless bodies – *and their dying screams were in German!*

Now the ones to the rear tried to fight their way out frantically as the dead piled up in a wall of bodies. The gunners didn't give them a chance. Fingers pressed to their triggers, they killed and killed and killed.

Sickened by that terrible slaughter, Schulze clamped his big paws to his ears, trying – and failing – to blot out those last cries in German.

Not far away, Petersen bit his bottom lip. He had heard them, too. Then he told himself that Schirmer had given him an order and that order was to knock the lone transport out of the glaring blue sky. 'Gunners – fire at will!' he barked, as he saw the Dakota's engines flash a bright red as the unknown pilot suddenly increased power. He had obviously spotted the slaughter taking place on the ground. 'Come on, don't let the shit escape!' he urged, 'or I'll have the eggs off'n the lot of yer with a blunt razorblade!'

The terrible threat had its effect. His sharpshooters swept the sky with tracer. It raced after the plane at an ever-increasing speed, a lethal white Morse of glowing slugs. Closer and closer it came. Petersen held his breath. The Dakota was picking up speed by the instant. Now he was making a determined attempt to escape, gaining height by the second, and Petersen could visualize the pilot sweating over the controls, mentally urging his plane to rise and evade that deadly fire.

But there was to be no escape for the unknown pilot.

Suddenly, slugs were ripping the whole length of the Dakota's fuselage. At that distance Petersen, mouth open in abrupt wonder, could see the bits of dark metal being torn off its sides and floating gently towards the desert, spinning like falling autumn leaves. 'You've done it . . .' he cried gleefully, *'you've done it!'*

Dark brown smoke started to stream from the Dakota's right engine. The prop feathered and stopped altogether and the crippled plane gave a crazy lurch. For a second, Petersen thought she was going to fall out of the sky altogether. But somehow or other the pilot caught in at the very last moment.

As the slaughter of the gliders came to an end, the volume of automatic fire giving way to aimed single shots, each followed by the death wail of yet another victim of that merciless slaughter, the Dakota began to go into a steep dive, followed by the white curve of tracer, the bullets bouncing, spent, off the plane's riddled sides like golf-balls.

'Cease fire!' Petersen yelled above the mad racket. 'Save your ammo . . . cease fire . . . That crate's had it . . . she's going to crash . . . *Cease fire!*'

The high-pitched hysterical burr of the massed machine-guns died away and there was no sound save the harsh satiated breathing of the gunners, the crackle of the over-heated barrels of their machine-guns cooling off, and that awesome splutter of a plane going into its terminal dive, like the gasps of a sick man fighting off death.

Petersen pushed his cap to the back of his head. The plane was no more than fifty metres from the ground now, thick black smoke pouring from both its engines, heading out into the desert to the south, out into that area that was marked on the map as a white featureless blank – uncharted territory. He wiped the sweat from his dripping brow. It couldn't be more than seconds now. The pilot didn't have a chance. The plane fell lower and lower. It had almost reached the burning horizon with its blue ripples of shimmering heat waves. 'Crash, damn you!' Petersen snapped suddenly, narrowing his eyes against the blinding sun. '*Crash!*' Abruptly he, too, was overcome by that mood of shame and anger that had attacked all the Headhunters as they stared at the slaughtered men, piled up like cordwood at the exits from the bullet-ripped gliders, knowing the men they had killed were German like themselves. 'Damn your eyes . . .*CRASH!*'

Minutes later, the plane had vanished over the horizon, leaving behind it the faint echo of that spluttering dying engine . . .

FIVE

Timmermann's nostrils were assailed by the stench of burning rubber. It ripped at his throat and made him cough and retch; it blinded him with tears. But he fought against the overwhelming desire just to lie back in his bullet-shattered seat and let it happen. 'What did it matter any more?' a little voice within him asked. 'I'm not shitting well going to die out here, damn it!' he roared back. 'Out here in the shitting middle of nowhere!' He grasped the controls, which shook like live things, in a fury, new strength surging into his limbs.

Next to him, young Sanders turned his head slowly, as if it were worked by rusty springs. Once he had been a very handsome young man in the stern blond Prussian fashion. Now he was a horror, one eye shot away leaving a scarlet suppurating pit, two dark holes full of pink-tinged mucus where his nose had been. But he was alive and conscious. 'Height fifty metres, skipper . . . air speed one-twenty,' he croaked in a cracked old man's voice . . . 'Port engine not functioning . . .'

Timmermann dared to free a hand for a moment. He patted the youngster on the knee. His hand came away wet with blood. Sanders' whole body had been riddled by tracer. '*Schon gut . . . schon gut,*' he whispered soothingly, 'I'll take it . . . Don't worry, I'll take it.' Hastily he looked away. Sanders was dying on his feet.

He concentrated on getting the crippled Dakota down. Ahead of him on the far horizon there was an area of red terrain, sandstone he guessed, firmer than the sand, especially with a shattered undercarriage. If he could only

belly her down there . . . Abruptly the Dakota yawned
alarmingly to the right. Shattered equipment slithered the
length of the plane. Bright fragments of broken Perspex
from the cockpit showered his face. The wind came rushing
in through the new hole in alarming fury. Timmermann
viciously kicked at the right rudder to raise the left wing.
Nothing happened. Timmermann cursed. Next to him,
the dying kid moaned. Desperately, he pulled back the
right engine throttle. The cabin was filled with the choking
fumes of escaping gas. The tank had been holed. In a
moment the Dakota might well explode in flames, but he
had to take that chance. He gunned the left engine at
maximum power. The fuselage groaned and howled like a
banshee under that terrible strain. For an instant the
Dakota halted its slipping – but only for an instant. A
second later the burning left wing flipped upwards alarmingly. With hands that were running with sweat, a terrified
Timmermann caught the plane before she slipped into a
final roll. The desert was racing up to meet them at a
horrifying rate.

'I just can't hold the pig!' he moaned through gritted
teeth, eyes bulging from his head with fear. '*Just can't!*'

'*Meine Ehre heisst Treue*,' Sanders called in his dying
ecstasy, '*Ich gelobe dem Führer Adolf Hitler . . .*' Lost in
some other world of long ago, Sanders repeated the oath of
loyalty to a leader who had been dead for a decade.

Horrified, Timmermann wished he could have placed
his hands to his ears and drowned out that terrible litany
of crazed death, but he knew he could not – he had to fight
the Dakota down. He had to!

Now the Dakota was only twenty metres above the
surface of the desert. The sandstone was coming ever closer
and he could make out the low wind-worn rocks, devoid of
any vegetation or boulders. He was going to make it.
'Come on you bitch,' he pressed his whole strength behind
the column, as if physically attempting to urge the crippled
plane on, his body lathered in a hot wet sweat now.
Suddenly she fell. This time he could not hold her. She

was going to crash-land in the desert. He held his breath, his hands frozen on the controls. Next to him, Sanders mumbled and mumbled, seeing nothing, hearing nothing but the voices of that other young, confident time in a Germany he would never see again.

The Dakota hit the sand with a sickening thump. A wheel broke and raced ahead of the plane as it rose into the air momentarily under the impact. Next instant it crashed down again, the whole undercarriage splintering terrifyingly. There was an appalling din. Propeller blades ripped apart, showering metal everywhere, the plane nosed into the sand, tossing sand to both sides in a great whirling yellow wave. The shock hurtled Timmermann forward with incredible violence. He yelped with agony as the shoulder straps cut into his flesh, ripping open his shoulders. A sudden fear flashed through his mind. If the shitting things didn't hold, his face would smash against the shattered cockpit, ripping it to shreds. He felt a searing pain in his right knee. Again he yelped with pain. Next moment, carried forward by its terrific momentum, the aircraft reared up on its buckled nose. For one agonizing second Timmermann was suspended in space, clinging on desperately, his ears full of that awesome sound of dripping gasoline. Trapped like this he could be burned alive!

Crash! With a roar like dull thunder, the Dakota slapped down onto the sand once again. A last jerk . . . Silence, broken only by the drip-drip of escaping gas and the hissing sound of glycol and gasoline vaporizing on the red-hot metal of the smashed engines. Suddenly thick white smoke started to seep in everywhere. He woke up to his danger. Shaking his head as if coming out of a deep sleep, Timmermann tugged himself free from the straps. He automatically switched off the engines, thus reducing the risk of fire.

'Quick!' he gasped urgently to his co-pilot. 'For God's sake, Sanders, let's make steam! Get the hell out of here . . .' He stopped short with a gasp of horror. Sanders lay back against his seat, dead, the broken shaft of the controls neatly impaling his heart.

Timmermann sat underneath the shattered wing carefully sipping the tepid water. There was still black market whisky inside the plane – he had intended to take it back to Berlin and sell it there – but he didn't drink it, though he would dearly have loved a slug. He knew it would burn him up worse than the sun which was now directly overhead, and besides, he needed to think clearly. Now he could not afford a single wrong decision. He knew all too well that there were no second chances this time; he had to get it right straight off.

According to his calculations, there was water enough inside the plane to last him four to five days, allowing himself two litres every twenty-four hours. If he weren't to dehydrate, he would need that amount. There was plenty of food, too, though that wasn't so important, in this heat, he told himself. There were weapons too – a Russian sub-machine gun, his and poor Sanders' pistol and a crate of grenades.

Timmermann wiped the sweat from his brow and tried to force himself to think his problem out. Basically, the question was how to get away from his mess with his skin in one piece? For he was determined not to die out here just for the sake of a bunch of ignorant slopeheads who wiped their arses with their fingers and who were going to be used by the Ivans for their own purposes. No sir!

He couldn't go north towards the coast. He had seen what had happened to the poor shits of instructors inside the gliders. They had been slaughtered without mercy. He could try to make it back to Egypt, of course, but he guessed that he would not be able to make the thousand or so kilometres to the Egyptian frontier with the limited resources still available to him. He stared at the red sandstone reaches, bathed a sinister blood-red in the blazing noonday sun. Somewhere out there were the slopeheads they had come to supply with weapons and instructors. At least they were supposed to be friendly and they *did* have contact with the Egyptians. If there was to be any hope at all for him in this merciless desert waste, it would be with them. He put down his water bottle and said, already beginning to speak to himself in the fashion of lonely men, 'Well, you old shit, it's got to be south, hasn't it? There's no other way.' He nodded his agreement and, rising, clambered back inside the wrecked plane, carefully avoiding looking at poor dead Sanders, transfixed by the broken column.

Half an hour later he was ready, food and extra water bottle stowed away safely in a haversack, Russian tommy-gun slung over his shoulder. He dipped the end of the roll of crêpe lavatory paper in the tank which supplied the port engine with fuel. Walking backwards he unrolled it until he thought he was a safe distance from the Dakota and applied the flame from his lighter to his end. Slowly the blue flame started to run the length of the gas-soaked paper, creeping ever nearer to the plane. He tensed, shoulders hunched automatically for the blow to come. Suddenly the gas tank erupted in a startlingly bright flash of blue, angry flame. He ducked as a piece of metal whizzed above his head; and then the plane was aflame, the greedy fingers of fire clawing their way the length of its fuselage. He caught one last glimpse of Sanders hunched over his shattered controls for all time, and then he, too, disappeared into the all-consuming flames.

He felt swamped by the realization that he was alone in this great desert waste, kilometres, thousands of kilometres, from his homeland and the few friends he had, facing not only a hostile nature, but foes, known and unknown. The thought pierced him like a sharp knife, yet in spite of his fears, his handsome if cynical face set in a look of firm resolve. 'Good-bye,' he whispered softly to the burning Sanders. For one moment he stood there hesitantly; then he shouldered his tommy-gun.

'*Auf los, geht's los,*' he commanded himself with the silly phrase they had used as children at the beginning of some race or other. He put his right foot forward and turned his face towards the south and that barren, baking unknown landscape that lay before him.

Behind him the shattered Dakota burned fiercely, tracer now beginning to explode like fireworks, zig-zagging at crazy angles in a fury of red, white and crimson in the hard blue sky. But Major Timmermann did not look back, for he had already forgotten the Dakota and the reason they had come here. Now, as he plodded ever southwards, a lone figure dwarfed by that immense cruel landscape, his mind burned with hatred and the desire for revenge. He knew he could go on for ever, in spite of the hostile environment, until he had made *them* pay for what they had done. His gaze concentrated on the sand at his feet, forcing himself not to look at the so-distant horizon, a trick of survival he had used many a time in the old days in the wastes of Russia. He neither saw nor heard the dark silhouettes of the motionless riders who were watching him with the patience of men who had all the time in the world in which to mount their attack . . .

SIX

In the twenty-four hours since they had ambushed the gliders, Schirmer's Headhunters had made satisfying progress across the red sandstone. The track they had been following had vanished and the going was rough, but there was no sinking sand or treacherous patches which had bogged the trucks down so often before. All day long they had made a steady ten kilometres an hour, guided by the sole slopehead who had survived Sergeant Tod's 'interrogation'.

The handful of desert tribesmen who had lived through the mad camel charge had proved a different breed to the city slopeheads. Skinny, swarthy, evil-smelling men, all endowed with great beaks of noses, they had let themselves be beaten to death by a furious, frustrated Tod until, finally, the last of them, a cross-eyed youth who could not have been more than fifteen, had broken. In a mixture of sign language, a few words of French and a torrent of unintelligible dialect, he had promised to lead them to the Red Oasis, actually going down on his knees, tears streaming down his swollen face to kiss Tod's blood-stained hand, when the latter had promised he should live.

Yet as Schirmer leaned against the wheel of his truck, savouring the evening coolness, which would soon turn to bitter cold, idly toying with his lukewarm cup of 'nigger sweat', he was worried. Ever since the slaughter of the gliders and the cries for mercy in their own language, his men had been overcome by a strange mood that he found it difficult to analyse; it was a mixture of self-disgust, apathy and latent hatred of their leader. For the first time since he had formed the Headhunters back in the dark days of 1945, he felt that his men not only distrusted him, but also disliked, even hated him. Even now as they prepared for sleep, crouching around their flickering fires of sand and gasoline, finishing off their evening rations, there was little of the animation that hot food and drink normally brought with it at the end of a long day; no salty stories about the exploits in the brothels of three continents, no hoary obscene soldiers' jokes, not even grumbling, a common practice among soldiers the world over, about their lot. Instead, they crouched near their fires in silence, and when they did speak, they did so in whispers, as if they were afraid of being overhead.

White Lightning appeared out of the growing gloom and sat down next to Schirmer with a sigh of relief. 'Good to get the weight off my feet, Colonel,' he said, gratefully accepting his own canteen of coffee. Schirmer had been keeping it warm for him over the fire while the big American completed his final round of inspection this day. 'Thanks.'

'Everything all right?' Schirmer asked, trying to dismiss the men's mood from his mind but failing to do so; he could almost feel it, it was so tangible.

'Sure,' White Lightning said easily, taking a cautious sip of the coffee, 'sentries posted . . . the lot.'

'And the slopehead?'

'Tod has chained him to the steering wheel of the command truck, Colonel,' White Lightning answered. 'Tod finds him too precious to let him get far out of his sight, so he's dossing down personally next to the Arab, though God knows how he stands the stink that's coming from the kid.' He laughed shortly. 'Boy, I don't think he's washed – *ever!*' He looked at Schirmer in the flickering blue light which hollowed out the colonel's features into a harsh death's head and his grin vanished. 'Problems, sir?'

Schirmer sucked his teeth hesitantly, 'I don't know really, Major, I just don't know. Ever since that business with the gliders . . .'

'You mean the fact that the guys we killed were German,' White Lightning said when Schirmer did not continue.

'Yes. Whatever the political opinions of those men, my Headhunters reason that they *were* German . . . And they don't like the way we slaughtered them – without a chance.' Schirmer frowned, as if finding it difficult to put his thoughts into words. 'And there's something else too . . . I can't really put my finger on it,' he added a little helplessly. 'It's this damned desert, I think.' He shuddered involuntarily although it was not yet cold. 'We've been in it too long. It's getting on the men's nerves – and mine, too, I must confess. It seems endless, as if we're slowly progressing to the edge of the world . . .' He bit his bottom lip and fell silent . . .

Schirmer couldn't sleep, although he felt exhausted after the long day. His mind refused to stay still. He tossed and turned on the cold sand, his brain a seething kaleidoscope of past and present. At two he gave up trying to make any attempt to get to sleep. Above him the night sky was brilliant, the stars harsh and silver, so close by that it seemed he could have reached up and grabbed one. All around him he heard the singing of the desert that he had become accustomed to by now: the contracting sand grains, rubbing against each other in the night cold and giving out a strange, haunting, eerie music.

He cursed and flung his Arab robe over his shoulders, his boots stiff and unyielding with the sudden cold. The camp was completely silent now as he plodded his rounds, shoulders hunched against the freezing wind that came from the desert. He passed the lead truck and saw Tod huddled in his blankets, sleeping on the ground next to the cab, chain extended stiffly to where his prisoner squatted inside. He sighed and wished he could sleep so soundly. The ex-Gestapo torturer seemed to have no imagination and no conscience. Life must be easy for people like that, he told himself, and passed on.

Now at this time of the night when younger men tended to doze off and neglect their duties, guard was taken over by senior NCOs – the 'graveyard shift', as they called it cynically, when human resistance was at its lowest and lonely frightened men began to imagine things. Schirmer slipped in beside Spider Arse who was sheltering behind a truck, staring into nothing, head hunched beneath his upturned collar.

Schirmer handed him a piece of hard candy. At night sentries were not allowed to smoke – their glowing cigarette ends could be seen for kilometres in the desert. Candy was the only substitute.

Gravely, Spider Arse thanked him in the soft voice that even the hardest of men seemed to adopt when on sentry-go in the middle of the night.

'How goes it?' Schirmer asked.

Spider Arse, the veteran of Stalingrad and Dien-Bien-Phu, did not take his gaze from the desert, as if he did not wish to look the man he had followed so loyally all these years in the face. 'Not so good, sir,' he answered in a day unemotional voice. 'I think the men have had a noseful.'

'A noseful of what, you old rogue?' Schirmer attempted to put a humorous note in his voice, but failed lamentably; the desert night was too sombre and oppressive.

'This, the lot!' Spider Arse flung out one hand, as if embracing the whole world. 'They're asking themselves what we're doing here, killing our own people – even if they *were* fighting for the Ivans – just so the Frogs can hang on to this particular arsehole of a place? I mean, sir,' he added a sudden plaintive note in his voice, 'what good is it? What good is the whole shitting place – and if it is any good like you say it is, then why aren't the Frogs out here, sweating out their guts, standing a chance of getting their outside plumbing sliced off by some murdering treacherous slopehead, sir?' For the first time he turned and stared up at the big, harshly handsome colonel, a look of naked accusation on his worn skinny face, hollowed out by the privations of the last days. 'Why, sir, *why?*'

But Schirmer was unable to answer that question, though he knew he would soon be forced to.

He stayed with Spider Arse a few moments more then he turned silently and walked back to his bedroll. Taking off his boots, he placed them carefully beneath his head so that his body heat would keep them from stiffening up too much by morning, and closed his eyes. Suddenly he was tired, very tired. Somewhere there was a Headhunter whispering. Sleep started to take hold of him. He thought he heard someone groan. He told himself that he should get up and investigate, but he had no strength. He told himself he must have been mistaken, for all was silent again. Next moment he was gone . . .

It seemed only minutes later that he was being shaken awake roughly. He blinked open his eyes; his eyelids felt as if they were pinned down with leaden weights. 'What . . . what is it?' he cried thickly through sleep-scummed lips.

It was Pansy Petersen, still in his hair-net, face stark and pale against the dirty grey light of the new dawn; and for once he was not inclined to his usual extravagant humour. 'It's the slopehead, sir,' he gasped, buckling on his pistol-belt as he spoke in urgent hectic gasps, 'he's gone and done a bunk!'

Schirmer sat up hastily and grabbed for his boots.

'Not only that, sir . . . They've done for Tod.' Petersen swallowed hard. 'Even Spider Arse, who found him, had to spill his cookies. It was that horri . . .'

'*Los!*' Schirmer cried urgently, not giving Petersen time to finish, a hundred conflicting and alarming thoughts racing through his brain.

Together the two officers ran across the stiff, frozen sand to where a group of shivering Headhunters stood around the cab of the first truck, while Spider Arse, one hand pressed out to support himself, leaned against its side, retching, retching, retching, as if he would never stop again.

Roughly Schirmer pushed his way through, crying, 'Come on . . . move it. Let me through now!'

He pushed aside the nearest man angrily and gasped with horror. An arm was hanging from the wheel of the open cab, suspended by a chain, and he didn't need to be told whose it was. The bloodstained camouflage sleeve could only belong to one of his Headhunters. He gulped, forcing back the hot bile that threatened to swamp his throat and said thickly, 'It's Tod, isn't it?'

Schulze, an ugly look on his brick-red face, snarled, 'Of course it is. That torturing pig has got his at last.' He spat angrily in the sand at his CO's feet. 'He deserved it. But we don't – and we're next if you ask me . . .'

'No one is!' Schirmer snapped, automatically noting the looks on the faces of the men all around him. They were at the end of their tether, he could see that. One wrong move now and they would snap. 'And watch your mouth, Sarn't-Major, or I'll have to stop it – for good!' He slapped his pistol holster significantly.

Schulze showed no fear. Instead he opened his mouth to say something else. Schirmer didn't give him a chance. 'Where's Tod's body?' he barked, 'and what happened to the prisoner?' He slapped Spider Arse hard across the back. 'You're the sentry . . . what happened?'

'There's Tod, sir,' one of the Headhunters said, 'or what's left of him.'

Forcing himself to do so, Schirmer, followed by Petersen and the rest, walked round to the other side of the truck. Stretched out on what appeared to be a blood-red carpet, lay the raw chunks of gory flesh which had once been Sergeant Tod. For all the world, they looked like the buckets of bloody offal and flesh that had stood in butchers' yards in Schirmer's youth. Someone had systematically cut the little ex-Gestapo man to pieces, taking his time about it, making sure that no limb had been missed. The murderer had even severed the fingers of the remaining hand, spreading them out in a neat fan of white flesh against the blood-soaked sand. It was the work of a fanatic, a madman, whose hatred was greater then his fear of being discovered.

'But how did they get away with it?' Schirmer stuttered, forcing himself to keep his eyes on that gory, grisly sight. 'He must have been slaughtered alive . . . He would have shouted the alarm . . .' He stopped short.

Gravely, his face set in a bitter look of suppressed rage, Schulze bent down and picked up what appeared to be a piece of dried red-brown leather from the mangled remains. 'He couldn't,' he said and Schirmer noted he didn't say 'sir', 'because they cut his shitting tongue out!'

Schirmer recoiled with horror, his face blanched under the sun-tan. What kind of madman could do such things, he asked himself, vividly visualizing Tod lying writhing on the ground, his mouth full of frothed blood, unable to cry out, as his murderers systematically sliced him to death, until finally he could stand no more and the spirit passed away from him.

'He deserved nothing better,' Schulze answered, tossing the tongue away with casual indifference. 'He died as he lived – by cruelty.'

'There are footprints over here, sir,' Petersen called, 'more than one set sir . . . leading towards the south.' His voice trailed away. No one was listening. All eyes were now concentrated on Schulze and Schirmer, the two comrades of a decade of war facing each other, faces set in bitter hatred, as if they had been enemies for all time.

Now there was no sound save the soft wind and Spider Arse still retching pitifully, his skinny shoulders heaving.

'We've got to go back, *sir*.' This time Schulze used the military courtesy.

'What!'

'You heard me, *sir!*' Schulze's voice was ominously even and without emotion. 'Or if we don't go back, then we should try to go west, make for Spanish territory. We could surrender to them and hope to get to South America eventually. Brazil, Chile, one of those places where they don't mind *our* kind.' There was a trace of a sneer in his tone for a moment. 'But we can't just go on. Because if we do, they'll get the lot of us in the end. We're too far away from the coast, our communications are shot – we haven't heard from Colonel Mercier for days now. We could all be dead as far as he is concerned. What hope . . . what purpose is there for us out here?' He ended, his voice level and steady, as if he had made up his mind and there was no changing it now.

Schirmer controlled his rising anger with an effort of will. Out of the corner of his eye, he saw Petersen and White Lightning furtively lift the flap of their pistol holsters. *They* were with him at least, but he had no intention of allowing this business to deteriorate into a shoot-out. That would be fatal. Then his Headhunters would really run amok. 'I understand your motives full well, Schulze, I can assure you of that. But you know my motives too, and why I think we should continue our fight out here. We know we're on the right track. This damned Red Oasis can't be more than forty-eight hours away now, and we've come too far to turn back at this stage. Let me put it like this, Schulze, give me forty-eight, let's get the job done by then. Thereafter, I promise you solemnly – even if we haven't found the slopeheads' camp – we'll set back for the coast once more. Now that's a promise.' He forced a grin and lowered his voice coarsely. 'And there'll be more gash and free suds than you could tackle in a month of Sundays!'

Schulze's features didn't change and his gaze remained wary. 'Sir,' he said slowly, 'it won't wash. We've heard it all before, those of us who are Old Heads at least. We heard it back in Russia in '43. Five years later you were saying the same things in Indo-China. It was no different at Dien-Bien-Phu the year before last. Now you're saying the same thing all over again here. And the youngsters come and get their turnips shot off and their guts blasted out, every year new cannon-fodder – dying for what?'

Suddenly there was iron in his voice and Schirmer knew that he was not going to convince Schulze this time. '*Pour la Gloire de la France?* Oh, my aching arse, is *that* worth a single German life!'

There was an angry mumble of agreement from the Headhunters crowded around the two opponents and Schirmer knew it could be only a matter of minutes, perhaps even seconds now, before the trouble started.

'But you must understand, Schulze,' he said desperately.

'I understand nothing, sir, except that this must stop. We've got to have a decision this very morning. There is no other way. This is the shitting crossroads for Schirmer's Headhunters!' he added, a pleading note in his voice. 'We can't go on any more, sir. *We've had it!*'

Schirmer looked at Schulze's broad honest face and his heart went out to him. Of course, they had had enough – all of them had, including himself. They were worn out. Some of them had been in combat for nearly twenty years; no one had seen so much fighting as they had done since the days of the *Landsknechte*[1] of the Thirty Years War. He was worn out himself.

Suddenly he recalled that last oasis with its Roman ruins, now almost swallowed up by the desert. Twenty centuries before, Roman centurions, far from their home-land, had manned those ramparts at the very edge of the world as they knew it. They had stuck it out four centuries. Then the rot had set in. Most of the legion had fled back to Rome, leaving a handful of centurions to defend this last lone outpost, perhaps as they had done elsewhere in Africa. It was said that these last defenders had nightly built great bonfires to make the wandering nomads, the Numidians as they called them, believe that the legions were still on guard. But year after year the Numidians discovered the same old trick and descended on fort upon fort, slaughtering the defenders. Perhaps that was what had happened in that lost oasis too. And why? Because of a lack of will, the resolution to fight to the last and not give

[1] German mercenaries of the 17th century.

in. They couldn't give in, too. There was too much at stake. First it would be Africa and then it would be Europe; thereafter the whole of what was left of the non-communist world.

Schirmer's face hardened. A nerve started to tic at his temple. He nodded to White Lightning and Petersen. They nodded back their understanding. Slowly and without any drama they slid out their pistols. In the heavy electric silence, the tension almost tangible now in the dawn air, both of them cocked their hammers. Schirmer's hand moved slowly but inevitably to his own pistol. He did the same, but he held the .45 down at his side. As yet he did not point it. 'Sergeant-Major Schulze,' he said in a formal, almost sad, voice, 'I am ordering you to resume your duties . . . *now!*'

Schulze did not move.

'Didn't you hear me?' Schirmer rasped, the sweat suddenly trickling down his face.

'I heard you,' Schulze answered in a level, completely calm voice, though Schirmer could see how the giant's hands trembled.

'Well?'

Schulze did not answer.

Deliberately, Colonel Schirmer raised his pistol. There was a collective gasp from the men. They started to draw back. At the truck Spider Arse stopped retching. 'I shall not talk any more, Schulze,' he said, quietly, 'I shall count to three and if you haven't gone back to your duties by then . . . then, I shall shoot you!'

Schulze appeared unmoved. 'Shoot me, as you wish, Colonel,' he said, his gaze fixed unrelentingly on Schirmer's face. 'But what then? There are five hundred odd of us. You *can't* shoot us all.'

'*Jawohl, ja!*' there was a growl from the men.

'If I have to, I will,' Schirmer said simply, raising his pistol so that it was pointed directly at Schulze's heart. 'Now I am going to start counting, Schulze.'

Schulze did not flinch. 'Then go ahead, if you can. It

will be better to die a clean death like this than what is waiting for us out there.' Suddenly he seemed to snap. His face flushed an even deeper red. 'What in three devils' names are you waiting for, man? Croak me, if you want, and have done with it,' he blurted out, his eyes abruptly blazing with a wild unreasoning anger.

Schirmer swallowed hard. '*One*,' he said huskily.

There was an angry murmur from the crowd of Head-hunters.

White Lightning and Petersen flashed each other an apprehensive look.

Schulze did not move, but his chest heaved in quick shallow gasps. Next to the truck, his running-mate Spider Arse had stopped retching. He had levered himself away from the truck's side, an unhappy, uncertain look on his face, but with his sub-machine gun now clenched in both hands. His gaze ran from Schulze's face to Schirmer's, as they confronted each other in the last showdown, and then back to Schulze's once more, as if he expected some sign, some command from the giant standing there.

'*Two!*' Schirmer hissed.

Now the angry Headhunters stared, fascinated, at the colonel's right knuckles, which whitened as he started to bring that final inevitable pressure on the trigger of his pistol. In one short moment it would start. There seemed no stopping it now. The Headhunters had come to the end of the road. If Colonel Schirmer killed Schulze, he would not survive more than five seconds himself. The massacre of the officers would then commence.

Schirmer swallowed hard. He twisted his head to one side, face flushed an angry frustrated purple, as if he were having great difficulty in getting out his words. He swallowed again. Schulze tensed, the look of rage in his faded blue eyes gone, to be replaced by one of pity and compassion as he stared at the man whom he had served so loyally – even lovingly – for so long, and who was now going to kill him. Schirmer opened his mouth, his finger taking that awesome last pressure on his trigger, 'Th . . .'

A single rifle shot rang out in that electric stillness with the impact of 88mm shell exploding in the old war. They turned, startled. Spider Arse was sinking to his knees with awful slowness, a star of bright scarlet growing ever larger on the front of his shirt. Suddenly his grease gun tumbled from his nerveless fingers and he slapped to the sand with frightening abruptness, dead, while they stared at him as if frozen thus for all time.

Schulze reacted first, as the clatter of flying hooves awoke them to their danger, '*Alarm . . . alarm . . . Zu den Waffen!*' he bellowed at the top of his voice, and even as he yelled his commands, his eyes told a transfixed Schirmer that he knew the game was up. There was no way back for the Headhunters now, any of them. The stage was set. The actors were in position. The final act could commence . . .

FLIGHT FROM THE RED OASIS

'What are the bugles blowin' for?' said Files-on-Parade.
'To turn you out, to turn you out,' the Colour-Sergeant said.
'What makes you look so white, so white?' said Files-on-
Parade.
'I'm dreading what I've got to watch,' the Colour-Sergeant
said.

R. Kipling: *Danny Deever*

ONE

The bare-foot Negro bowed. One by one, he started to kiss a dazed Timmermann's fingers, while the cross-eyed youth who had been his guide since his surprising rescue grinned for some reason known only to himself. Timmermann, his hair and eyebrows bleached almost white by the last forty-odd hours in the desert sun, let it happen. He was too weary and too bewildered to do anything else.

The welcoming ceremony apparently over, the big turbanned Negro indicated that Timmermann should take a place in the shady entrance of the cave. Gratefully, Timmermann sank down on the palm fronds placed there and wiped the sweat from his brow. All around him the ragged children looked at each other as if the movement was of some significance; while their mothers, shrouded in black from head to foot, dark-brown hands tattooed with blue signs, holding their veils to their faces so that only one eye, heavy with kohl make-up, was free, stared down at this weary white stranger with unblinking concentration. Next to him the cross-eyed youth, whose face was still swollen from the beating his captors must have given him, pointed to a pile of what looked like fritters which had been placed there and made a sort of shovelling movement. 'Mangez,' he commanded with one of the few French words he knew.

Dubiously, Timmermann took one, while the Negro, crossed-leg on the ground now in front of the cave, started an elaborate ceremony, pouring hot water from a copper kettle into a tea-pot, adding a sprinkling of green tea-leaves and then spoonfuls of coarse brown sugar. Time after time he poured a little into a cup, tasted it, made loud disapproving noises with his big brilliant white teeth, and returned the contents of the cup to the teapot.

Timmermann let him get on with it. It was another slopehead game as far as he was concerned. His main interest was the place where he now found himself: thick groves of dusty palms set around pools of fairly clear water that he judged came from deep, deep below the surface of the ground, surrounded by ancient caves dug into the sides of the red sandstone with, here and there, black tents pitched among the trees.

There were men and animals everywhere, seemingly lazing around while their black-clad womenfolk did the work, hauling the water from the springs, cooking over fitful little fires set at the doors of their caves, beating the tough flesh of old camels with clubs to make it more palatable – and all of them were armed. Timmermann let his gaze sweep across the oasis as far as he could see and judged there were upwards of two thousand men present, some carrying great curved rifles over their shoulders dating back to the nineteenth century, others armed with more modern German, British and American rifles, the loot or cast-offs, he told himself, of the great battles that had raged in this part of the world in World War Two. He instinctively knew that these were the people they had flown from Egypt to supply with arms and train in their use. He supposed that they were his friends, though most of them had such fierce cruel eyes over their great beaks of noses that he felt they would put a knife in a man's back almost as casually as a good German burgher might cut a piece off a cold roast of pork.

The Negro finally seemed satisfied that he had done full justice to the rite of showing this white guest that no trouble was too much for his hosts. Ceremoniously, he handed a cup to Timmermann and then another to the cross-eyed boy who had accompanied him across the desert to this remote oasis, after the roving band of tribesmen had freed him. Timmermann sipped it and grimaced. It tasted like a sweet cough syrup. But his companion was delighted and gulped down his tea in one go and held out his cup for more. A second cup was poured and Timmermann was forced to take one from the Negro, who was all teeth – he seemed to have more than anyone else the German pilot had ever met – as he added mint to this one. Happily, the cross-eyed boy savoured this one more slowly, drinking it with loud sibilant sips, obviously to show his appreciation.

Timmermann frowned, his strength – and impatience – beginning to return now after the long trek. Why were they – whoever they really were – wasting so much time with this ridiculous tea business? Didn't they know that a whole battalion of killers were advancing this way and the handful of tribesmen who had stayed behind after the rescue hadn't a hope in hell of holding them up with their antiquated rifles? The German legionnaires, for he knew now from the boy that they were German, would slaughter them mercilessly. The men who peopled this oasis would have to take defensive measures soon, or they would be overrun. Timmermann's sunburnt face contorted at the thought and an angry nerve started to tic at the side of his face. The bastards had to be paid back for what they had done and it was only through these primitive slopeheads with their damned herbal tea that he could ensure that that happened. '*Himmel, Arshch und Zwirn,*' he cursed to himself, 'when are they going to get down to damned business?'

The great thudding of horses' hooves that suddenly alarmed the crowd of women and children watching the tea-drinkers in the cave seemed to come as an answer to his unspoken question. The spectators hurriedly fell back to both sides. Skinny-ribbed dogs ran away, tails between their legs. Sheep and goats bleated. Sand rose in a cloud as the horsemen came galloping into the oasis at full-tilt, waving their weapons, crying wildly, robes flowing, dark faces crazy with excitement. For one moment, Timmermann thought they would overrun the tea-drinkers, including himself. But, as if at some unspoken command, the horsemen reined, as one, digging their heels into the gleaming flanks of their mounts, pulling cruelly at their bits so that they cavorted on their hind legs, whinnying and yelping with sudden pain, their riders holding on proudly, the silver-encrusted trappings jingling.

Timmermann's two companions hurriedly rose to their feet and began to bow as a strange kind of heroic dirge rose from the desert riders, punctuated at intervals by weird cries and much threatening with their rifles. Down at the oasis, the excited camels took up the racket and began to snort. Donkeys and dogs, not to be outdone, started to bray and bark. Now the women and barefoot children joined in, uttering shrill, birdlike cries, whooping like Red Indians, clapping their hands to their mouths. Everyone and everything had become overcome by an uncanny, barbaric excitement.

Then, as abruptly as it had started, the dirge ceased. As one, the hundreds of riders wheeled their steeds round. In a great cloud of dust they raced away, goading their horses into a wild thundering gallop, digging their ugly silver spurs into their mounts, leaning down low over their flying manes, firing their rifles into the air as they pounded across the desert and disappeared into the distance. Behind, they left a little group of elderly Arabs, dressed in white, their silver daggers and short curved swords glistening in the slanting rays of the late afternoon sun. Slowly, very slowly, Timmermann began to rise to his feet as the group started to trot towards him, their swarthy faces set and inscrutable. He was in the presence of power; he knew that instinctively.

Caid Abd el Kader ben Mahoudi waved away the Negro with the tea with an imperious gesture of his skinny claw, not taking his black eyes off Timmermann's face for one moment, as if he were trying to see something in the German's eyes that only he would be able to recognize, while the sheiks grouped around him waited for some pronouncement.

Timmermann felt himself begin to blush. There was something embarrassing about his old man's penetrating, unblinking scrutiny. He had not felt like this since his days as a naughty *Volksschüler* brought up in front of the *rektor* for some offence or another. He wished the old boy with his long flowing white beard and skinny face, wrinkled like ancient leather, would end the long silence. Outside there was no sound save the drone of the flies skimming over the heaps of droppings left by the galloping horses.

Suddenly the Caid smiled, his black eyes almost disappearing in a sea of wrinkles, revealing long white yellow teeth, sharpened, or so it seemed, like the fangs of some wild animal. Leaning forward, he pressed Timmermann's knee and said in clear, if hesitant German, 'You are a friend . . . You came to help us.'

Timmermann's amazement at the fact that this desert nomad living a thousand kilometres away from civilization could speak German must have been apparent; for the old man said happily, 'My son, the oldest, the one who is now dead. He learned your tongue. He taught me some . . . enough.'

'Of course, of course,' Timmermann said happily, knowing now that he would be able to inject some urgency into his discussion with these remote slopeheads. 'You speak very good German, sir. Now sir, you know about these men from the Legion advancing on—'

The Caid held up his hand for silence. 'For the time being,' he said, 'they are being taken care of, German. My riders will hold them long enough for us to plan.'

'To plan, sir?' Timmermann echoed stupidly. 'But they have most modern weapons, trucks, perhaps even some sort of artillery.' He ran out of words and stared incredulously at the Arab who thought he could hold up a well-trained battalion of German mercenaries with their antiquated muskets.

The Caid was quite calm. 'Yes, they have modern

weapons, by friend,' he said slowly. 'I will grant you that. But we have the desert and,' he paused, as if he were searching for a word, 'our cunning . . . They will come to us, full of European pride and superiority.' He looked momentarily at Timmermann with such naked barbaric directness that, in spite of the heat of the late afternoon, the German shuddered involuntarily, 'but, I can assure you, they will never return . . . now this is what we shall do.' He bent forward and began to draw a line in the sand with his dagger . . .

TWO

'*Shit, shit, shit!*' Colonel Schirmer cursed, as he ducked and yet another slug whacked into the sand only millimetres from his head. 'There can only be a handful of the brown bastards out there – and they've got a whole battalion of Headhunters tied down!' He frowned and tried not to listen to the cries of the Headhunter dying nearby in what had now become no-man's-land between them and their unknown assailants.

'*Mutter,*' the dying man wailed piteously, '*Mutter, lass mich doch nicht hier sterben!*'

White Lightning flashed a look at Schirmer. The latter nodded. Soon the sun would slip beneath the horizon, and both of them knew what these desert tribesmen would do to the wounded man out there in the dark. Tod had been enough.

'Petersen,' White Lightning, commanded, 'spray my front. They'll think I'm gonna make a run for it.'

'One . . . two . . . *three,*' Petersen counted off. He raised himself and whipped a furious burst to left and right.

In the very same instant White Lightning raised himself too and took careful aim at the wounded Headhunter writhing in the sand some fifty metres ahead of them. 'One . . . two . . . three . . . four,' he called aloud, as he pumped slug after slug into the soldier and then ducked, as the Headhunter's body contracted in its death throes and the Arabs hidden in the red rocks to the right began firing at him. The cries for 'mother' ceased.

'Good,' Schirmer said in a dry monotone. 'Thank you,

Major. The men don't . . .' he didn't complete his sentence.

'*Christ on a crutch, if it was raining shitting gravy we'd be the shits with ferking forks,*' Schulze's voice thundered. '*Let me get at them shitting slopeheads!*'

'*Schulze!*' Schirmer cried in vain.

The giant sprang to his feet, his face brick-red with rage. He waved a steam-shovel of a fist in which he clenched the rifle taken from a dead Headhunter. 'Come on, you pack!' he shrieked at the men pinned down behind the dunes, 'do you want to live for ever? *Forward!*' Not waiting to see if they followed him or not, Schulze darted forward, zigzagging crazily like an American football player heading for a touchdown, bullets kicking up spurts of sand at his flying feet.

All the tension of that long day released now, the Headhunters streamed past Colonel Schirmer and White Lightning, discipline thrown to the winds, strained sweat-lathered faces set in wolfish grins of sadistic pleasure. The first line was scythed down by the Arab fire. But the second line came on, howling like demented banshees, falling and stumbling over the bodies of their comrades – but still going on.

The Arabs started to break. Here and there, a white-robed figure rose from his hiding place in panic and started to pelt for the camels tethered in the wadi beyond. To no avail. Now the Headhunters were among them. Schulze spotted an Arab coming straight at him and fired a bullet from the hip. The Arab went down howling. As Schulze ran on, he smashed his boot into the dying man's face. Another Arab loomed up. Schulze pressed his trigger. Nothing happened. His magazine was empty! The Arab's rapacious dark face broke into a smile. He raised his rifle. Behind Schulze, Petersen pressed the trigger of his automatic. Schulze could feel the heat of the slugs hissing by. The Arab screamed piteously. Suddenly he was a dwarf, both his legs sawn off at the hip. Schulze swung his useless rifle like a bat. The butt connected and the Arab sailed over a dune backwards as if he were a human ball.

Petersen went down, shot in the knee, cursing furiously at his own bad luck, his grease gun tumbling from his sweating fingers with the shock of the sudden pain. Schulze stopped and looked back. 'Trust an officer,' he gasped, his great chest heaving, as if he had just run a race, 'go and get hissen shot just when the fun starts—' He stopped short. Two Arabs were racing for the kneeling man, curved knives upraised. 'No you don't, you brown slopehead shits!' Schulze yelled. He darted back.

The leading Arab thrust at the big man. Schulze parried the blow with his rifle. Next moment his right boot lashed out and slammed into the Arab's crotch. He reeled to the ground, his scream of agony drowned in his own vomit.

The second Arab veered to the right. Too late. The butt of Schulze's rifle smashed into his skinny dark face. Bones splintered cruelly. Thick scarlet blood jetted from his nostrils, mouth and ears, mingled with the brilliant white of bone splinters. He went down without a sound.

Now the Headhunters were among the Arab line. There was no room for manoeuvre and it was every man for himself. Steel against steel. Knives and shovels flashed in the intense white light of the sun. Bayonets, gleaming like silver, slashed. Men, white and brown, swayed back and forth, locked in an embrace of death, gasping and grunting as if in the last throes of sexual ecstasy. Below their shifting feet, the dead and dying were trampled into the sand. No quarter was given or expected. It was a fight to the death.

Schulze grabbed the bayonetted rifle of a dead Head-hunter just in time. An Arab rushed him, dark eyes crazy with excitement, curved sword upraised. The blades locked with a clash. Schulze grunted contemptuously. 'Wet slope-head fart,' he growled between clenched teeth. 'Tit-sucking greenhorns can do better than that back at the depot!' With an easy, practised twist of the wrist and a heave from his right thigh, he smashed the Arab's sword to one side. It fell to the sand. The Arab screamed, shrill and hysterical, like a woman. He cowered there, hands raised to his face, as if he could not bear to see what was going to happen next. Schulze lunged. His bayonet penetrated the Arab's stomach. He howled and tried to pluck the cruel blade out. Schulze didn't give him a chance. He grunted hard and thrust it ever deeper, until the gleaming-red point came out of the man's back and he sagged dead onto the blade. Schulze aimed a savage kick at his skinny guts and the bayonet came free with a horrible sucking sound. The Arab crumpled to the blood-stained sand and Schulze blundered on.

Another Arab broke. Howling as if demented, he raced for the bleating camels, rearing up in fear, their mouths covered with froth. Schulze spotted him. 'No, you don't,' he roared and raced after him. 'There's gonna be no left-overs from this particular little picnic!' The Arab saw his pursuer. Eyes crazy with fear, he stopped for an instant and threw his knife, his sole remaining weapon. Schulze yelped with pain as the knife gouged a long piece of flesh from his left shoulder before tumbling to the ground. 'Why, you little slopehead shit!' he bellowed and increased his pace.

The desperate Arab bolted for the excited, terrified camels and grabbed for the nearest hobble. Too late – Schulze was upon him, red-enraged lights flashing off and on before his eyes as he raised his bayonet. The Arab tried to bury himself into the sand, while the camels started back and forth, splattering foam from their ugly mouths. Schulze plunged home his weapon. It went clean through the Arab's body, transfixing him to the ground. The camels reared up on flailing hooves, narrowly missing Schulze's shaven skull as he tugged desperately at the weapon, trying to free the bayonet. It wouldn't come out. 'Shit on the shingle!' he roared, beside himself with the unreasoning rage and blood-lust of battle, while the camels flailed the air all about him. He grabbed for cartridges and inserted them in the breech with fingers that felt like sausages. He pressed the trigger. The rifle erupted and the back of the dead Arab's skull exploded. A gory spray of blood and broken bone shot upwards. The camels had had enough. They broke their tethers. As Schulze sank to the ground, his bayonet freed, next to the headless victim, they raced madly across the desert, accompanied by the waning snap-and-crackle of the dying fire-fight. The battle was almost over.

'Well if this is all the slopehead shits can put up, what are we worried about?' Schulze said contemptuously, spitting out date seeds, and thrusting another bunch of the looted fruit into his big mouth with fingers that were caked with black blood right up the knuckles.

Next to him, White Lightning put his boot under one of the Arab corpses and turned it over. The flies which had already begun to feast off the dead man's sightless eyeballs rose in an angry cloud. 'One lousy cutlass,' he said aloud, assessing the man's equipment, 'and what looks like a blunderbuss. I bet it doesn't have a range of more than fifty metres – with any accuracy.'

Colonel Schirmer frowned, watching his happy, exhausted men looting the dead who were sprawled everywhere in the scuffed sand. At that moment, his mood was a mixture of pleasure and worry. He was pleased that this easy victory over the Arabs who had pinned them down most of the day had restored the confidence of his Headhunters; there would be no more talk of turning back now. The mutiny had died a quick death. On the other hand, he didn't like the sudden euphoria which had overcome his men now that they had seen at first-hand the quality of the opposition and the poor state of their equipment. Over-confidence, he knew well from nearly twenty years of combat, led all too often to defeat and disaster. Hadn't that been the case in Soviet Russia back in '41 and '42?

As the red ball of the sun started to sink slowly over the horizon and the deep black shadows began to race across the desert towards them, Schirmer made up his mind. The Arabs knew, of course, where they were by now. The men they had defeated were merely a raiding party, and there would be more of them. If he were to complete the mission that Colonel Mercier had given him what now seemed an age ago he would have to keep the enemy off balance. But how?

For a few moments he considered his next step, although in his mind he already knew what had to be done. The Headhunters had to vanish – as of now – before a new raiding party was sent out to attack or shadow them. He realized it would be a decision that his Headhunters wouldn't like, after a day of being pinned down under that murderous sun. He stared at their worn, tanned faces. They looked as if the very juices had been drained from them, just as the colour had been drawn from their uniforms and boots by that tremendous heat, so that the leather was now a pure white and the cloth faded and almost colourless. Could he impose any further strain on men who were already so hard-pressed?

'A lot like this,' Schulze's happy voice boomed across the desert, 'I could tackle with my eyes closed and one hand tied behind my back! Great crap on the Christmas tree, one shot from my fart-cannon and I'd do for the lot of them!' He raised his right leg and loosed a tremendous, explosive stream of wind.

Schirmer grinned softly. They'd be all right, he told himself. They'd do it, even if they had to roll all night long before they abandoned their trucks and made the final approach march to the Red Oasis on foot. *His* beloved Headhunters wouldn't let him down. He hesitated no longer. Drawing out his whistle, he loosed three shrill blasts on it.

They had rolled all night, steering by compass and the tracks of the panicked camels, since Schirmer guessed they would have returned to the Red Oasis (if indeed that was

where they had come from); the tracks clearly outlined in
the sand by the hard silver light of a myriad stars. The sky
was beginning to flush an ugly white to the east and
Schirmer knew it would soon be time to hide the trucks
before beginning the last stage of their mission on foot.
'We can assume they'll be waiting for us,' he had told
White Lightning and Schulze a little earlier. 'That cross-
eyed devil who got away will have told them we're coming.
So we can't run the risk of just walking into a trap.
Somehow or other, we have to catch them off guard and
use our superior firepower against their numbers to the
best effect.'

'A night attack?' White Lightning had suggested.

'Tricky, sir,' Schulze had added an instant later. 'You
know the kind of mess-up that can be made at night?
Besides, it lowers the advantage we have in firepower.'

'Agreed, agreed,' he had answered. 'But I'm not taking
any chances on this one, you big rogue. We've come too
far, been through too much. I want to bring the Battalion
back the way it went in.' He had glanced at the others'
faces reflected by the green light of the instruments in the
windscreen, looking like sombre starved ghosts. 'I don't
know how to say this, comrades. But I think the days of
the Headhunters are numbered . . .'

They had looked at his reflection in the windscreen,
aghast, and he had nodded dourly. 'Our day is done. This
will be the last mission of Schirmer's Headhunters and it
is going to be a mission with as few casualties as possible.
We've spilled enough German blood for France's colonial
empire. Time are changing. Perhaps . . . perhaps, we can
go back after all?'

Now, as the horizon grew lighter and lighter, Schirmer
recalled those words and felt his jaw tightening with
resolve. They *would* do what they had come to do – but
they were not going to pay the kind of butcher's bill they
had paid in the past. Not this time! His Headhunters were
going to survive this one.

One hour later, as the sun coloured the sand the hue of

bright red blood, the shadows of the trucks cast stark black and hard and they ground to a halt. Schirmer found the place he needed to hide them: a large wadi, enclosed on three sides by red sandstone cliffs with a narrow entrance that could easily be defended, if necessary, by the handful of men and the wounded he intended to leave behind to guard the vehicles and prepare them for the long haul back to Beni Abbes. One by one, the trucks drove in while Schirmer, followed by Petersen and White Lightning, clambered up to the heights to survey the terrain ahead with their glasses.

The landscape was bare and as inhospitable as ever, kilometre after kilometre of featureless red sandstone, already beginning to bake in the morning sun, the heat waves shimmering and trembling in blue lines above it. Expertly, the officers ran their glasses from left to right, covering the ground very thoroughly, for they knew of old that seemingly open ground could hide a large number of trained men. But they could see nothing. The desert seemed empty.

Schirmer lowered his glasses slowly. 'By now, gentlemen,' he said, 'we could have expected to have overtaken the camels at the speed we were going, so we can assume that they have arrived back at this damned Red Oasis. We can conclude, therefore, that the place cannot be very far beyond that horizon. I suggest that we let the men rest till dusk. Then we will march under cover of darkness – we'll spot their camp fires more easily at night. My aim is to be in position for a pre-dawn attack. I don't want to make it complicated. Just to take-out their leaders, if we can, give them a damn good bloody nose, without casualties on our part, and then back here *at the double!*' he laughed at the phrase. 'Very much at the double!'

The others laughed, too. Schirmer made it all sound so simple – and safe. The strain and worry of the last few days vanished. Now they knew what they had to do and Colonel Schirmer appeared so confident and relaxed. Nothing *could* go wrong.

'Sir!' Schulze's voice cut into their reveries from below. '*IT'S COLONEL MERCIER, SIR . . . WE'VE GOT HIM ON THE RADIO, SIR!*' Schulze shouted through cupped hands. '*COME DOWN, QUICK!*'

Mercier's voice was faint and distorted, but there was no mistaking its enthusiasm and happiness as Schirmer pressed the earphones to his head in the bakingly hot truck interior, lit by the little orange light of the radio. 'Great news, my dear fellow, great news!' he called. 'We've gone into Egypt at six o'clock this morning.'

'*We?*' Schirmer queried in bewilderment.

'Yes, the French, the English and the Jews. Our paras have already landed and are seizing Port Said. Everything is going splendidly. Even the English are moving. This is a real war now, Schirmer, and it's the first time we've had allies since 1945. Tomorrow we strike for Cairo and once there we'll hang that rogue Nasser from the highest building in the whole damn place. It'll be the end of this whole dirty business in North Africa. Without aid from the Egyptians, the FLN will fall apart. So, my dear Schirmer, deal with those desert chiefs and that'll be an end to it.' Schirmer could almost sense Mercier's mood of triumph back there at the coast over a thousand kilometres away, as the little Frenchman's mind raced at the prospect of victory after ten long, bloody years of disastrous colonial wars. The rot had stopped. France's colonial empire would be saved after all. 'Do you know what Cairo means in Arabic, Schirmer?' Mercier's voice crackled over the ether.

Schirmer shook his head, as if he were actually facing the Frenchman.

'I shall tell you. It is from *El Qahirah*, the Victorious. Tomorrow, Schirmer, or at the latest the day after tomorrow, we French will be the victors there,' he chuckled suddenly, 'and you and I can retire to some grey foggy township in Lorraine, next to the dear General[1] to spend our remaining days boasting of the past, trying to get up the skirts of the local widow women, and drinking ourselves

[1] General de Gaulle, who had exiled himself to Lorraine at that time.

to death in splendid fashion, what? ... *BONNE CHANCE, SCHIRMER ... OUT!*'

Schirmer laughed outright, his sweat-lathered face more relaxed than it had been in many a year. Mercier was right. The death of Colonel Nasser would bring the various anti-revolutionary movements all over the Middle East tumbling to the ground in ruins. He sat back and, handing the dripping earphones to the puzzled operator, wiped the sweat from his brow. Now he knew everything would go well on the morrow. This was going to be the last time for him and his Headhunters. He'd retire and write his memoirs. He sat up suddenly and crooked a finger at a waiting Schulze.

'Sir?' Schulze barked, as if he were back at some pre-war barracks in the old Reich.

'I've got some good news for you, you old sauce-hound,' Schirmer cried happily.

'Sir!'

'Stop shouting "sir" like a shitting wooden soldier,' Schirmer exclaimed in high good humour, 'order the wine ration to be broken out. One litre per man. Let them get as high as a house. They can sleep it off all day.'

Schulze stared at him, open-mouthed. 'A litre ... of wine ... but ... but ... why, sir?'

'Because we've got a victory to celebrate, you big horned-ox,' Schirmer yelled exuberantly, 'a victory at last ...'

THREE

'It's just like June, '41, sir,' Schulze whispered softly, as they crouched there in the pre-dawn gloom, watching the numerous dying fires flickering fitfully among the trees of the oasis. 'Remember that night just before we crossed the Bug? God, weren't we tense! Nerves going like fiddlers' elbows – and the blokes getting up all the time to go and have a piss with tension.'

Schirmer, lying on the rocks next to the big NCO, grinned and rubbed his unshaven chin, wishing that he had shaved beforehand after all, in spite of the shortage of water. It seemed somehow fitting that he should go into his last battle washed and cleanly shaven, as befitted a soldier who had once been a member of Hitler's elite. 'Lot of water flowed under the bridge since then, Schulze,' he whispered.

'Yes,' Schulze agreed, 'a shitting oceanful of it, if you ask me! Think of all the lads who have gone hop since that day, divisions of them, the poor shits. Buried all over the shitting place and their widows living high on the hog on their army pension. Up the cups – and up the shitting skirts, too, I shouldn't wonder,' he added, a trace of bitterness in his voice.

Schirmer didn't speak for a moment. Suddenly he had a vision of long ghostly battalions of young soldiers marching by him, their dead eyes staring at him silently from ashen-white faces in bitter reproach. Yes, indeed, how many young men had died since that pre-dawn attack on Soviet Russia at 3.30 on the morning of 22 June, 1941! 'Well,' he said, trying to put a light note on it, 'Sergeant-Major Schulze is still with us – whether that is a blessing or not, that is not up to me to say.' He grinned at Schulze and Schulze grinned back. 'Some say, good old Sergeant-Major,' he repeated the old quip in the Headhunter Battalion, 'and some tell the truth!'

Petersen crawled cautiously through the rocks, filled with waiting men, and dropped down next to the colonel. 'All in order, sir,' he whispered. 'One and Two Companies are in position on both sides of the oasis and our tame American has set up a stop-line on the far side just in case they get some idea of trying to make a breakout there once the balloon goes up.'

'Sentries?' Schirmer snapped.

'They've got a couple guarding their camels and horses,' Petersen replied. 'Typical slopeheads, though, they're all sawing wood. Fast asleep.'

Schirmer nodded his thanks. 'Seems almost too easy,' he commented. 'I suppose they didn't expect us to get here this soon.'

Schulze frowned like someone who has just remembered something not very pleasant, but he said nothing.

Schirmer flashed a look at the soft velvet of the night sky, then at the green glowing dial of his wrist-watch. 'All right, Petersen, this is the plan. Take Three and Four Companies and work your way down to the centre of the oasis – towards that patch of palms and larger tents at twelve o'clock. If their leaders are sleeping anywhere, it'll be there. Don't try to form a skirmish line – the ground is too broken for that. Let the men go in in twos and threes. Once you're clear of the rocks, form up. When you're ready, fire a white flare and go in *fast!* I shall then fire a green flare to alert our tame Ami and One and Two Companies. Hit them hard and hit them fast. Then come out the same way you went in. Don't wait for stragglers. We'll cover them.' He paused and frowned. 'Anyone too seriously wounded to keep up and who could endanger his comrades, well you know what to do, Petersen, we can't allow any of our fellows to fall into the hands of those murdering bastards.'

Petersen nodded with unusual gravity for him and made a clicking noise with his forefinger as if pulling the trigger of a pistol.

'Yes, shoot them,' Schirmer snapped shortly. 'Pull through to us and set off straight away for the trucks. One and Two Companies will fall back at five minute intervals. Headquarters will cover them and be last out, since we're not going to be actively engaged in this – er – little brawl. Got it?'

'Got it, sir.' Suddenly Petersen's old flamboyant style broke through in spite of the seriousness of the situation. He touched his lips with an affected gesture and simpered, 'How do you like my lipstick, sir? Don't you think it's a most delightful shade. Goes well with my tan, I feel.'

'Away with you, you awful naughty girl,' Schirmer laughed. 'Pull this one off and I'll buy you a hair dresser's salon for your retirement!'

'Oh, la, la!' Petersen flipped a limp wrist at the big colonel, 'wouldn't that be fun? All those lovely youths in their tight trousers – a veritable honeybums' paradise!' And with that he swayed away. Schirmer would never see him again.

Now the two companies under Petersen's command began to move out, dodging from rock to rock on the descent in little groups, socks pulled over their boots to cut down the noise, bandages wrapped round their bayonet scabbards and metal rifle slings to reduce the clatter of metal on rock. Here and there a man cursed softly as he dislodged a few pebbles or slipped on the slick surface of the red sandstone, and Schirmer kept flashing nervous glances at the silent oasis below. But nothing stirred. Even the camels, nervous animals in spite of their phlegmatic appearance, made no sound. The tented camp slept on, the only sound the last crackling of the dying fires. Schirmer told himself happily that it looked as if they were going to achieve complete surprise on this one.

'The last mission, sir,' Schulze whispered softly, putting his thoughts into words, 'and this time we're not going to be caught with our drawers down around our ankles.'

'Right in one, Schulze, thank God,' Schirmer agreed heartily. 'Now then, get ready.'

'We're poor little lambs who've lost our way,' White Lightning hummed happily under his breath, while all around him his machine-gunners tensed behind their weapons, *'baa . . . baa . . . baa . . . Gentlemen-rankers out on a spree. Damned from here to Eternity . . . God have mercy on such as we . . .'*

'Sir,' the nearest gunner hissed. 'White flare at twelve o'clock!'

White Lightning forgot the song. *'Baa . . . Yah . . . Bah!'* he intoned hastily and looked straight ahead beyond the silent oasis. A white flare hung in the sky, glowing eerily, bathing the desert floor in its unnatural gaudy light. He swallowed hard and told himself it wouldn't be long now. 'Stand to,' he said softly, 'and check, the lot of you, check you're on automatic. Pass it on!'

The command ran the length of the line, while White Lightning waited tensely for the next flare which would signal the real start of the operation, that old jingle of his college glee-club days still running maddeningly through his mind: *'Damned – from here to Eternity . . . baa . . . baa . . . baa . . .'*

'Green flare, sir!' the nearest machine-gunner reported, the excitement all too evident in his voice, as the second flare sailed into the sky and exploded above the oasis with a soft plop. Abruptly everything below was bathed in its sickly light. White Lightning whipped up his night glasses. Had the enemy been alerted at last? Swiftly he swept the tents with them, and breathed a sigh of relief. Nothing . . . absolutely nothing stirred. Even at the animal lines all was silence. The place could have been uninhabited, yet he had seen the dark figures of the Arabs outlined by the fires earlier on; and even now he could just make out the strangely rigid figures of the sentries guarding the camels and horses, leaning on their rifles, obviously fast asleep.

He lowered his glasses and flashed a look at his watch. Five minutes to go. Grinning at the oasis, upon which Petersen and his killers would descend so rudely in a few minutes, he whispered to the darkness, 'Good luck, Honeybum!'

Petersen grinned to himself and flicked back the hammer of his .45, as his men formed up on either side of him, doing so without any command, for they were veterans, who had done this kind of thing many times before. He wondered if his old company had still been alive – which they weren't – what they would have thought of their former commanding officer now, dressed as he was in ladies' silk knickers under his uniform, with his lips painted and a hefty squirt of eau-de-cologne under each shaven armpit. During those days back in '42 when his had been the most feared anti-partisan *Kommando* in the whole of the Ukraine, any self-confessed homo, even if he had been awarded the Knight's Cross by the Fuhrer himself, would have speedily found himself behind 'Swedish curtains' – if not worse. But that had been long ago, he told himself, as he crept forward with his men, all of them with their bodies slightly bent, as if they were advancing against a strong wind. In this year of 1956 anything went. 'The spirit of the age,' he whispered to himself, a look of cynical contempt on his painted, knowing face, 'anything goes'.

'*Follow me, lovely boys,*' he said aloud as they came level with the central tents. '*Remember, the lieutenant's got a hole in his arse!*'

Like grey wolves, emerging from the night to snatch their unsuspecting prey, they crept closer and closer to the tents, damp fingers tensed on the triggers of their weapons, breath coming in sharp, short gasps, nerves jingling electrically. In only a matter of seconds now they would be discovered and the slaughter would commence . . .

*

Colonel Schirmer anxiously flashed yet another look at his watch.

Schulze said softly, 'Don't worry, sir. Everything's going all right. That Lieutenant Petersen is a careful one, in spite of his – er – disability.'

'Disability!' Schirmer grinned in spite of his anxiety, 'well that's a nice way to put it. If the Fuhrer only knew!'

'If the Fuhrer only knew.' Schulze echoed the old well-remembered phrase from the war and grinned, too.

From down below there came the clank of something hard and metallic being struck. Schulze's grin disappeared. 'What's that?' Schirmer rapped. 'It sounded like—' the rest of his cry of alarm was drowned by the sudden, well-remembered obscene howl. A spurt of scarlet flame split the darkness. A mortar bomb streaked upwards from beyond the oasis and began to plummet down on the tent area at a tremendous rate.

'A mortar, I didn't order any mortar fire!' Schirmer yelled frantically in the same instant that he realized with a sickening feeling of betrayal that something had gone wrong – seriously wrong.

'*Nicht schiessen, Kameraden!*' the German voice cut into the startled silence that had followed the explosion of the first bomb in the oasis. '*Wir sind Freunde.*'

White Lightning spun round, as the next mortar bomb shot into the sky and came hurtling down right into the ranks of Petersen's stalled companies. 'What the hell is going on?' The cry died on his lips.

White robed figures were rising from the folds in the ground behind them everywhere, like dead men rising from the grave. There must have been hundreds of them, and immediately in front of them stood a white man, tommy-gun cocked casually over his right arm. White Lightning caught his breath in surprise. The white man held up his hand to prevent White Lightning from speaking as yet another bomb exploded below and the loud echoing silence was shattered by the thunder of many flying hooves and the wild excited cries of men attacking the oasis from all sides. 'Surrender,' the man cried, 'it's your only chance . . . *surrender now!*'

'*Surrender!*' White Lightning exploded. He instinctively grabbed his pistol and fired from the hip without aiming.

Timmermann yelped with pain and dropped to one knee, his kneecap shattered. 'You murdering bastard!' he shrieked and fired.

The tommy-gun rattled at his hip and White Lightning was caught by a burst in the stomach. It ripped the length of his guts, stitching great ragged holes along the flesh – holes which immediately filled with blood and shit. His hands fanned the air, as if he were climbing the rungs of an invisible ladder, then he was down on his knees fighting death to the last – to fall under the bare feet of the Arabs who rushed forward to swamp his stop-line . . .

Now the mounted men were swarming over the oasis. The mortar barrage that had caught the Battalion by surprise had stopped and the slopeheads were flooding in every-where, screaming their war cries, waving their swords above their heads in hysterical triumph. The night air was heavy with the stink of burnt cordite, as the trapped Headhunters backed away, firing from left to right, felling their attackers by the score. Still they kept coming on, a confused mass of men and beasts, a solid wall of flesh.

Petersen, already wounded in the left arm and thigh, bent down on one knee next to a group of senior noncoms, firing controlled bursts at the howling mob as coolly as if they were back on the range at Algiers. Petersen wasn't afraid. Indeed, he felt exhilarated. Furious adrenalin coursed through his every nerve. His eyes seemed particu-larly keen and his mind worked with fantastic speed and clarity. He knew they hadn't a chance, but somehow he was not afraid. He would die here, that he realized. There'd be no barber's shop for him, with delightful young 'Figaros' in tight black trousers. He was fated to die here in this God-forsaken place, whose very name he did not know. Yet the knowledge did not scare him. Perhaps he had always half-expected to go this way. Now he raised himself as best he could, supporting himself against a bullet-pocked palm and screamed with tremendous elation, 'Knacker the slopeheads, men . . . Remember you're the Headhunters . . . *Schirmer's Headhunters . . . FIRE . . . FIRE . . . FIRE!*'

He pumped burst after burst into the surging mass of horses and riders, cutting great gaps in their ranks, with the shattered beasts writhing on the ground, flailing the wounded with their flying hooves as they thrashed about in their death agonies.

But still the slopeheads kept on coming, urging their horses forward with cruel digs from their spurs, lashing their sweat-lathered, trembling flanks with their reins, foam flecking the mouths of both riders and mounts as they came in for the kill.

'*A la baïonnette!*' Petersen screamed. He clubbed his useless grease gun and waited.

The ragged circle of survivors, their ammunition beginning to run out now, fixed their bayonets and waited as the Arabs recoiled and prepared for the last charge.

'Petersen's last stand!' the lieutenant cried crazily, his eyes gleaming like those of a madman, as he raised himself to his full height.

'*ALLAH!*' the screech went up from the ranks of the horsemen. They thundered forward, hundreds of them, swords upraised, crouched low over the flying manes of their terrified horses. The Headhunters fired their last bursts. Riders and horses went down on all sides, severed flesh flying under the impact of that terrible blast at such short range. Horses went down, whinnying piteously. Others raced on riderless, or dragging their stirrup-trapped masters with them through the bloody carpet of dead bodies. The thwack of slugs into the bodies of men and mounts was clearly audible above the pounding of hooves.

'Here we go!' Petersen yelled and swung his grease gun like a bat. An Arab went flying from his mount. Petersen ducked and his terrified bay sprang cleanly over his head. Next instant Petersen yelled with overwhelming agony as a sword sliced deep into his shoulder. The grease gun tumbled from his useless arm. He dropped to one knee again, the blood jetting scarlet from the terrible wound. A sergeant tried to reach him, swinging his bayonet from left to right. He didn't get far. An Arab tugged at his bit. His frantic, terrified mount reared high in the air on its hind legs. For what seemed an age, man and mount were poised there like some heroic equestrian statue that Petersen remembered from the little village squares of his youth. '*To me, the lieutenant's got a hole in his arse*,' Petersen chortled weakly, the strange red mist that had appeared from nowhere threatening to engulf him at any moment. The Arab brought down his curved sword with a tremendous swish. The sergeant screamed. The force of the blow was so terrific that he seemed to be split right down the middle. He dropped without a sound. Petersen giggled. Then he was on the ground. Men and horses were shouting and galloping all around him. Somehow it didn't seem to matter any more. He was dying and he was glad.

A coarse, hook-nosed, swarthy face, framed by a flowing white head-dress, towered above him. He glimpsed a brass-bound rifle butt being raised. His face was going to be smashed in. He waited, almost patiently.

But a beringed skinny hand, wavering in the red mist, pushed the rifle aside. A hand groped for his loins. Idly he wondered what was happening. The sensation was vaguely pleasant. He felt his trousers being opened and his nostrils were assailed by the sweet perfume of women. Suddenly fear surged through his dying body. He tried to scream, but he couldn't. They had loosed the women onto the survivors – and he knew what Arab women did to prisoners!

He heard the women gasp when they discovered his silk knickers, trimmed with French lace. They were ripped off – perhaps exhibited, he did not know. All he could hear was harsh sadistic male laughter and the giggles of women. Then a dainty hand took hold of his member. He tried to pull away, but he couldn't. He heard the gritty sound of knives being sharpened against stones. And then, as the woman tugged at his member, he felt the first cold touch of steel against his shrinking organ. Now he screamed . . .

The remaining Headhunters were stumbling, blundering through the lines of the Headquarters Company, eyes wide, wild and staring, mouthing meaningless words, wounded exhibiting their bleeding flesh, as if in justification, as they streamed behind the waiting Headquarters men.

Schirmer, standing there with his drawn pistol next to Schulze, stared down at the massacre below, horror-stricken, feeling the small hairs at the back of his shaven neck stand erect as he listened to the screams, the piteous pleas for mercy, the agonized bellows of his men down in the oasis.

'It's their women!' Schulze said through gritted teeth, eyes sick with horror, 'they've turned them loose with their knives, sir! *Oh, God in heaven,*' he retched suddenly, supporting himself with his free hand against a rock, his big shoulders heaving as if he were sobbing.

Below them, the screams went on and on, accompanied by the strange warbling cries of triumph made by the women, as they emasculated man after man; and Schirmer, standing there waiting for the last of the survivors to get through, could visualize them holding the gory, red-dripping bits of severed flesh and gristle aloft before tossing them away, dark rapacious faces set in expressions of contempt.

But there was no time to dwell upon that now. They had walked straight into a trap. The tents had been empty, the figures of men guarding the horselines had been dummies. They had attacked a deserted village, with the murdering swine of tribesmen hidden outside all the time, just waiting for them to walk in and be slaughtered. Now he had to save what was left. 'Schulze,' he commanded above the shrieks and the last wild shots as the remaining Headhunters fought to the end, 'knock it off, man! There's no time for that now . . . We've got to move back to the trucks!'

Schulze looked up, eyes filled with tears, vomit running down his unshaven chin, 'We haven't got a chance, sir!' he sobbed. 'We'll never make it . . .'

'Shut up!' Schirmer interrupted his moans brutally. 'We've *got* to make it. You know the slopeheads? They'll celebrate their victory. There'll be the usual orgy of mutilation of my poor fellows, then the looting and the squabbles over who gets what. They'll occupy themselves for an hour at least, fighting over who'll get the weapons they've captured and trying them out – only when all that business is over will they start out after us. They'll assume we're the survivors of that bloody mess down there, easy pickings.'

Schulze pulled himself together. The CO was right, of course. The slopeheads didn't know that there were still some well-armed Headhunters of the Headquarters Company left, who had not been engaged in the battle for the Red Oasis. He frowned suddenly. 'But they've still got the advantage of their nags and those shitting ugly camels of theirs, sir,' he protested.

'I know, I know!' Schirmer snapped testily, as if Schulze had reminded him of something that he preferred to forget. 'But we'll just have to do the best we can. Delay them till the first bunch of those poor devils who have just passed through get to the trucks. They can return and pick us up.' He frowned heavily. 'From now on, Schulze, we have to live up to every letter of our Battalion motto. From here on in, it's *march or croak!* Come on, let's go!'

Schulze took one last look at the oasis below. The sun was beginning to turn the leaves of the palms a deep crimson, outlining in stark black the dying men below, swamped by the hordes of slopeheads. '*March or croak*,' he whispered with unusual softness for such a big, loud man. He touched his hand to his bare head as if in salute. '*Auf wiedersehen, Kameraden*,' he whispered and then he, too, had disappeared into the glowing shadows of the new day . . .

FOUR

It was furnace-hot. Above, the burning sky was a leaden, threatening grey. Not a breath of wind stirred and the air was as stifling as the inside of a Turkish bath. A storm was brewing, Schirmer knew. All the signs of the *khamseen* were there; and for once he hoped that it would come soon. For it was, perhaps, the one thing that might save them before their pursuers caught up with the weary, panic-stricken survivors of the massacre at the Red Oasis.

It was clear that the Headhunters had reached the end of their tether. The track the survivors had taken before them was littered with abandoned equipment, tunics, kepis, even weapons; and the rearguard had twice come across gravely injured men who had fallen out, unable to keep up any longer. For them there had been no hope and, sending the others on, Schirmer had remained behind to administer that last bullet, the *coup de grâce*: the muzzle of his pistol placed at the base of the dying man's skull, a slight hesitation, a quick pressure before jumping back hurriedly as the skull shattered, sending blood and bone flying everywhere.

They crawled through that vast empty landscape like a trail of insignificant black ants and Schirmer, bringing up the rear with Schulze, told himself that the very countryside breathed hostility. Never had he felt so alone and so threatened. Time and time again, he tried to resist the temptation to look behind and see if they were already being followed – and failed. Each time the desert had been empty of those black figures on horseback he half-expected to see, but soon, he knew, they *would* be there – and then the end would not be far off.

'Christ, if only the damned storm would break, sir!' Schulze cursed, wiping the sweat off his crimson bull-neck with a dirty rag. He glanced up at the sun, a moody copper-coloured ball in the seething grey heavens, eyes narrowed to slits. 'Give us a shitting chance at least!'

Schirmer nodded and spat out the pebble which he had been sucking to save using water and keep the juices flowing in his parched mouth. 'Yes, it's our only hope, though I wonder about those poor fellows up there in front of us. I've got a compass bearing on the place where we hid the trucks, but I don't know about them.' He frowned. 'In the *khamseen*, they could walk within fives metres of the place and not see it.'

'I know, sir, I know. But now it's every man for himself,' Schulze said. 'The Headhunter Battalion is finished, wiped out, kaput!'

Schirmer sadly nodded his head in agreement and stumbled on.

An hour later the hot, damp-clinging breeze which indicated the onset of the sand storm at last started to ripple the surface of the desert, whipping up sudden sand devils, little flurries of dancing sand that erupted and died the very next moment, when they spotted what they had been expecting all along: a group of riders, perhaps six or seven of them, stark black silhouettes against the burning horizon.

'Shit,' Schulze cursed, gripping his machine-pistol more tightly in a sweat-damp hand, 'now the clock's definitely in the bucket!'

Schirmer flashed a look over his shoulder at them and then at the sky. They were too few to attack his column – he knew the Arabs, they needed overwhelming superiority of numbers – but they would soon ride away to inform the others. The burning question was whether the storm would hit them before the main body of their pursuers attacked. Suddenly he started to pray like he had never prayed before. If they ran out of luck this time, none of his poor fellows would ever see their homeland again.

The enemy scouts had split up, a decision which Schirmer cursed, for they'd lead the main body to his shattered force quicker that way. Twice already Schulze had stayed behind, feigning death in the hope of ambushing the three riders trailing the rearguard; but both times the riders had stayed well out of range, and in despair Schulze had fired angry but pointless bursts at them.

The weary Headhunters, strung out now over half a kilometre or more of desert, struggled on, crimson faced, panting, their shirts black with sweat, casting anxious glances over their bent shoulders, followed by others at the sullen sky. But the sand storm stubbornly refused to come and Schirmer, now the last man in the column with the Arab scouts only five hundred metres away, recalled the old Arab saying: 'Death is a black camel which knocks at every man's door.' Soon, he told himself, face set and grim, those black camels would be arriving in their hundreds and that would be the end. *God in heaven, why didn't the damn storm come?*

It was half an hour later – still without the expected storm, although it was becoming hotter by the second – that Schulze groaned, 'Visitors, sir, I'm afraid.'

Schirmer swung round, his heart in his boots, and hurriedly focused his glasses.

The blue-rippling horizon was crowded with dark shapes, silhouetted there against the leaden sun like some classical frieze. But there was nothing beautiful about this picture. The deadly intent was almost tangible. Schirmer dropped his glasses and spun round, wildly searching ahead for some kind of defensive position. Nothing save flat featureless desert, with here and there patches of camel scrub, some of it already torn loose by the wind and fitfully wafting back and forth across the sand. He cupped his hands about his mouth. 'Assemble at the shrubs at ten o'clock,' he bellowed. 'Do you hear me, men, assemble there . . . at the double!'

'We haven't a chance in hell, sir,' Schulze said wearily as the men began to run heavily for the camel scrub, as if their legs were made of rubber.

'I know . . . I know,' Schirmer answered miserably. 'But we'll go down fighting, taking a few of the bastards with us . . . and we'll each save the last bullet for ourselves. There's going to be no repetition of what happened back there at the oasis.'

Schulze nodded his head grimly in agreement and then the two of them were running after the rest.

'*ALLAH!*' the dreaded cry came wafting across the desert behind.

Schirmer flung a glance over his shoulder. 'They're going to charge, Schulze!' he yelled. 'For God's sake . . . *run!*'

'*ALLAH . . . ALLAH!*' The thunder of racing hooves was all too clear now. The very ground seemed to tremble beneath them as the two men ran for their lives. Suddenly a strange mist started to spring up, cloaking the men in front of them in its wet shroud so that it could be only a matter of moments before they sank into it altogether.

Schirmer's heart leapt with joy, in spite of that dread thunder coming ever closer. It was the *khamseen* – the sand storm was beginning! He could feel its hot wet fist begin to buffet him as he ran.

'Look out, sir!' Schulze shrieked in alarm.

He spun round. A rider was racing for him full-tilt, only a hundred metres away. Schulze's machine-pistol hissed. The rider shot clean over the head of his mount and slammed into the sand. They pounded on, the wet mist growing thicker by the second, the roar becoming ever louder. Now they could hardly see the fleeing men in front of them; it seemed as if they were running through billowing clouds, the outlines black shadows reflecting on them. But the Arabs were almost upon them. Now they were everywhere in the fog that preceded the *khamseen*. A rider loomed up directly ahead of Schirmer. The big, panting colonel fired without aiming. The man screamed and dropped unconscious over the steaming neck of his horse. It reared up with terror and then it was off, carrying the dying rider with it.

Schulze blundered into Schirmer, the sand particles already clinging to his sweat-lathered face so that he looked as if he were wearing a yellow mask. 'We'll never make it, sir!' he roared above the howl of the wind. 'Get down here, dig in and let the shits overrun us! They're too intent on the oth . . .' He fired wildly and an Arab was bowled from his horse in mid-gallop. Schulze did not wait for an answer. Instead he pushed Schirmer to the ground, just as three other riders broke from the howling mist. '*Dig!*' he hissed, '*for* God's sake – *quick!*' Kneeling there, he snapped off three sharp shots. Two of the Arabs went down without a groan. The other swung his horse round savagely and galloped away into the gloom.

Frantically, the wind tearing at their clothes now, camel-thorn rolling by in flying bundles, the two of them shovelled away the sand with their hands, flinging themselves into the shallow pits that they had dug there, as the sand storm descended upon friend and foe alike.

Then all else was forgotten but naked survival as the *khamseen* raged, gusts of wind threatening to rip them out of their narrow graves, the particles of flying sand striking their bare faces with lethal ferocity. Time and time again they opened their mouths to howl with the pain of it all, but the great hot wind snatched the cries from their mouths, leaving them gasping for air.

Time was forgotten. Now the world was simply one great hellish fog of sand. Anarchy reigned. It was each of them for himself. The rest of the Headhunters – the enemy – were all forgotten now. Nothing mattered save the task of surviving the elemental fury of the storm. It was a naked, uneven battle between man and nature . . .

*

Schirmer raised a hand. It was heavy with sand. It dropped in a shower and somehow he fumbled in order to find his goggles. He rubbed them clear and sat up with an effort, his ears still ringing with the echo of that terrifying storm. He blinked, feeling the gritty sand particles in his eyes. Cautiously, he rubbed them with his knuckles and tried once more.

The desert was transformed. Its surface gleamed and rippled with bright new sand: and it was completely empty. The Headhunters had vanished, just like the Arabs who had pursued them. Schirmer's mouth dropped open. It seemed as if he was alone in that vast wasteland, completely alone. He moaned like a trapped animal, an elemental piteous cry that came down from deep within him. There was no one left. *He was alone!*

Groggily he staggered to his feet, the sand falling from him in cascades. He stumbled round, eyes narrowed in the slanting rays of the afternoon sun. But peer as he might, the desert remained obstinately empty. He sank to his knees, wringing his hands, broken at last. He, Erwin Schirmer, was the last and only survivor of the whole battalion. Five hundred men had entered the desert at Beni Abbes and now he, alone, was left.

'God,' he cried, raising his head to the sun, hands clasped in the classical pose of supplication, 'don't leave me out here . . by myself!' he pleaded in a broken voice. 'Please . . . *not* by myself . . . anything but that!' The tears of self-pity started to stream down his face, tracing little rivulets through the caked sand, as he rocked from side to side on his knees.

'Sir.'

Schirmer stopped his moaning. He turned slowly, still on his knees, as if his head was working on rusty springs.

'Yer original chocolate-coloured coon in person,' Schulze said with a huge grin, wiping the sand from his face as he emerged from his 'grave', two large circles marking where he had removed his sand-goggles. He winked knowingly at his beloved CO, as if he had not seen the tears, the look of hysteria on Schirmer's face. '*Unkraut*[1] *vergeht nicht, was?*' He winked again.

Somehow Schirmer managed to wink back and echo that familiar old, hoary phrase and then the two of them were clasped in each other's arms, slapping one another on the back, talking excitedly, the tears streaming down both their faces now. *They had survived the holocaust. They were going to come through . . .*

[1] Literally: 'weeds don't die.'

FIVE

They stumbled upon the four dead Headhunters an hour
later. They had been mutilated, their eyes gouged out,
their throats slit in a ragged, jagged line, with their flies
torn open to reveal cruelly tortured lower bodies. Crazed
as they were for water, the two men hardly noticed. They
turned the bodies over brutally and, with trembling fingers,
searched frantically for the dead men's water bottles.
'One,' Schirmer choked and tossed it to Schulze.

Greedily, the big NCO unscrewed the cap and, throwing
back his head, drank and drank, while Schirmer searched
for a bottle for himself. He found one and, not even seeing
the tortured young man from whom he had taken it, he
threw back his head too and felt the delicious sensation of
water trickling down his parched throat and the saliva
beginning to function once more. 'My God, was that good!'
he sighed, wiping the back of his hand across his mouth,
his lips a sudden red against his sand-caked face, as if they
had been painted with lipstick. Carefully, very carefully,
he closed the water bottle and started to check for more.

Schulze stood guard, new energy and resolution flowing
through his dehydrated frame. Behind them on the horizon, the thick black clouds of oily smoke ascended to the
sky; the Arabs had discovered their trucks and were now
busy burning them. Although they had not discussed the
matter, neither of them had expected to make it to the
vehicles before the Arabs. Both had known instinctively
that that particular escape route had been blocked.

Schirmer looked up and raised his loot for Schulze to

see. 'Two canteens of water,' he said slowly, 'a can of old man,[1] one hundred francs, three pornographic photographs of ladies doing something improbable with a donkey – and these,' he indicated the little cartons in front of him on the sand.

Schulze laughed softly, 'Holy strawsack,' he said, half in admiration, half in wonder, 'Parisians![2] would you believe it – Parisians in the middle of the goddam Sahara Desert! What did the poor shits think they were going to snake out here in this wilderness?'

'What indeed!' Schirmer said a little sadly. Routinely, he bent over and closed the man's eyes. 'Now he'll never need those again,' and he made as if to toss the packets away.

Schulze grabbed his hand. In all seriousness, he said, 'Hey, sir, don't throw them away. *We* might need them! You never know, we *could* meet a camel!' He looked straight at his CO's lack-lustre, red-rimmed eyes, forcing him to smile, willing it with all the strength of purpose left in his big frame. And he succeeded.

Suddenly Schirmer sat back on his heels and began to laugh. 'Why, you big rogue,' he gasped, 'Of course . . . we'll make it!' He wiped the tears from his eyes and said, 'Schirmer's Headhunters are not finished yet.'

'Of course they're not.' Schulze tapped the water bottles with more confidence than he felt. 'These little beauties will last us at least five days, if we ration ourselves. With a bit of luck we'll find that Hannibal track again by then. Perhaps we might bump into some friendly slopeheads to take us back to Beni Abbes.' His jaw hardened, 'And if the khaki-coloured shits are not friendly, I'll make them friendly – right toot-sweet!' He clenched his big steamshovel of a fist significantly.

'I believe you, Schulze, I believe you,' Schirmer said, holding his hands in front of his face, as if to ward off a blow. Then he rose to his feet and flung a last glance at the

[1] Tinned meat reputedly made out of old men.
[2] Contraceptives.

trucks burning on the horizon. 'Well, let's hoof it, Schulze, while they're still occupied.'

Obediently, the big noncom 'hoofed' it.

It was on the morning of the third day that they saw the truck far off to the north, trembling and distorted in the heat haze. For what seemed an age the two men, their faces brick-red from the exposure they had suffered, noses burnt and peeling, their eye-brows bleached a bright white, stared at the vehicle, as if they could not believe the evidence of their own eyes until Schulze choked, 'It can't be a mirage, sir . . . 'cos there's no dancing girls nor little green fellers!'

The absurd remark broke the spell. Hurriedly, like men who were within grasping distance of the Holy Grail itself, they set off, stumbling, arms reaching out, muttering incoherent crazy phrases, occasionally breaking into a ragged trot until their strength gave, their brains racing, inane grins on their worn faces. Suddenly Schulze came a halt.

Schirmer nearly blundered into him. 'What is . . . it?' he gasped angrily, 'why . . . why did you . . . stop, you idiot?'

'Sir,' Schulze contained his hectic breathing with difficulty, 'that's . . . that's not one of our trucks . . . I can see that . . . from here!'

'Don't talk rubbish!' Schirmer began, shading his eyes against the glare and peering at the lone vehicle, which was stationary, and realizing that there was no sign of any Headhunter near or in it.

'I'm not talking rubbish, sir,' Schulze said, wiping the sweat from his forehead. 'Look at its shape. They ain't made trucks like that since I was as high as three cheeses . . . That's a pre-war truck, believe me.'

Again Schirmer opened his mouth to protest, but thought better of it. Schulze was right. The lone truck did have balloon tyres similar to their own, but the similarity ended there. Its shape was definitely that of another age. Besides, the vehicle was strangely weathered, the colour almost vanished, its canvas roof bleached a bright white, as if it had been there a long, long time.

Slowly, their enthusiasm and energy vanished, as if a tap had been opened and it had drained out in a rush. They came closer and closer until they could make out its details more clearly, from the curved snouts and tyres attached to its side, down to the fact that it was buried up to its axles in sand – and there were no tyre marks on the floor of the desert beyond.

Schirmer looked at Schulze, but there was no enlightenment to be found on his face; he was just as bewildered.

They paused at the nearside door. Cautiously Schirmer reached out and tried the handle, its paint long gone to show the dull gun-metal beneath. It came away in his hand to reveal the jumble of rags and bits of paper on the floor within, mixed with the sand which had sifted in from below. Schirmer picked up a piece of newspaper, which flaked almost immediately in his hand, it was so brittle. But he did manage to see the name *Le Monde* and the date before it did so: '*Avril, 1937*'. He whistled softly and turned to a still-bewildered Schulze. 'Do you know this thing has been here nearly thirty years, Schulze?'

'But how could that be, sir?'

Schirmer shrugged. 'This dry desert air and the sand, I suppose. They preserve things very well. This one was probably part of some long forgotten Trans-Sahara operation. In the twenties and thirties the French went in for that sort of thing in a big way.'

'But where . . . where are the fellers who were in it? Their bodies?' Schulze queried.

Five minutes later they found the answer. A mere fifty metres or so away they came across two grinning skeletons, attired in bleached white rags, beneath what looked like the remains of a shelter-half, attached to camel scrub and weighted with stones, large empty old-fashioned water bottles hanging from the twigs explaining all too clearly what had happened. The two Frenchmen had followed the usual advice given to desert explorers to remain close to their vehicle, which could be more easily recognized from the air. But no one came and finally their water had run out.

Schulze abruptly sat down with a weary groan. It was as if the sight of the skeletons exemplified all too clearly what their own fate was going to be, sooner or later . . .

Schirmer had the idea while they sat at the back of the bleached truck in the shade it afforded from the heat of the midday sun, idly munching some of the 'old man' smeared on a cracker he had found in the truck. 'You know there could be a way out,' he said slowly and hesitantly, as if he did not dare broach the subject, even to himself.

Schulze looked up wearily, a light of defeat in his red-rimmed eyes. 'Way out-what?' he said listlessly.

'Like this.' Before a suddenly enraged Schulze could stop him, Schirmer had risen and poured one of their precious bottles of water into the open radiator of the truck.

'What in three devils' names did you do a damnfool thing like that for?' he demanded, springing to his feet, fists clenched angrily, chest heaving.

'Because the beast will need some water – if we're going to start her, Schulze.'

'*Start her!*' Schulze cried. 'The engine's as dead as a dodo!'

'There you're wrong. I got a faint spark – and, my dear Schulze, there's at least half a tank of gas left. Enough for – say – two, three hundred kilometres. The sun didn't evaporate all of it.'

Schulze's angry look vanished to be replaced by one of bewilderment. 'But if they had gas, why did they die out here?' He indicated the two grinning skeletons.

'Can't say. Something went wrong and in the end they drank the water out of their own radiator. Perhaps they thought they'd be rescued from the air. Who knows?' He shrugged. 'All I know is that if we can get her started, we stand a fighting chance of getting close enough to Beni Abbes to make the rest of the way in a day's march on foot.'

Schulze's face lit up. 'Do you really think so, sir?' he asked, new energy in his voice, hope flickering across his face.

'The air's awfully dry here in the desert. She should fire easily, even if the battery is almost dead.' He turned and pointed to the slope to the right of the truck. 'See that rise, Schulze?'

The other man nodded wearily.

'It's about fifty to seventy metres high . . . with a corresponding drop on the far side. Now, Schulze, if we could get her up there . . .'

'Up *there*, sir? Christ on a crutch, she must weigh half a shitting ton!'

Schirmer ignored the outburst. 'Get her to the top and give her a good push-off and we might *just* start her. I know, I know,' he added hastily, seeing the doubtful look on the other man's face, 'it would be nip-and-tuck . . . But what other alternative do we have?'

A heavy silence followed, while Schulze considered and Schirmer waited anxiously; for he knew that if Schulze refused to help him, there was no hope for them. Sooner or later their bleached bones would join those of the long dead French explorers.

Schulze slowly rose to his feet. Idly, or so it seemed, he kicked the nearest tyre of the stranded truck. It withstood the kick easily. He did the same with the other three, while Schirmer followed his every move. Suddenly he turned, a grin on his worn face, 'All right, Colonel, I'm on,' he said. 'Might as well drop dead of a heart attack trying to push that whore's son up the hill, as sit here on my big keester, melting away.' Drily he spat in his big palms, 'Colonel, when do we start?'

SIX

They dug solidly for an hour, in spite of the murderous heat, using the spades they had found in the truck, giving themselves no rest, their upper bodies glazed with sweat, their shirts wrapped round their heads in a poor attempt to ward off that killing sun from the backs of their skulls.

Schirmer knew they should rest – at this rate their bodies would dehydrate too rapidly – but neither he nor Schulze had the patience to slump in the shade. Time was running out. Both of them knew that instinctively. They were desperate to discover whether the truck which hadn't run for nearly thirty years could really start. Almost immediately, they set about trying to move the truck up the slope.

Schirmer slipped behind the wheel and yelped as his hand touched the red-hot metal of the big brake handle. It refused to budge, but after he had belaboured it a couple of times with the shovel, it moved. Next he whipped off his belt and tied the wheel down so that it would not be forced from the central course by the sand and make their gigantic task even more difficult. Finally he thrust the gear into neutral. He looked at Schulze. Schulze nodded. Wordlessly they took up their agreed positions: Schulze to the rear, his massive back braced against the tailboard, Schirmer next to the doorless cab, his shoulder lodged against the front right mudguard. '*Eins . . . zwei . . . drei . . . heyrup!*' he called, as farmers do when they attempt to get a bogged-down cart out of the mud, and took the strain with a grunt.

Nothing happened.

'*Once again!*' Schirmer grunted. '*Los!*'

Again they heaved with all their strength. There was the crack of splintering wood. Schulze cursed as his big shoulder burst one of the rear panels and he almost lost his balance. Suddenly the truck lurched. There was the rusty squeak of wheels moving that had not moved for three decades. 'The whore's son!' Schulze cried excitedly, *'moving! Keep it up, sir!'*

They heaved and strained for a solid hour, their breath coming in sharp gasps, their shoulder muscles burning as if on fire, hearts beating agonizingly, as if they might burst the confines of their rib-cages at any moment.

By that time they had advanced ten metres and, as Schirmer hurriedly pulled the handbrake and Schulze jammed two handy rocks behind the rear wheels before they both collapsed into the sand, the way ahead looked as steep as Everest to the exhausted men.

They started their self-imposed torture again fifteen minutes later, toiling up that murderous incline, pants black with sweat, muscles ablaze, swaying from side to side like drunken men as they pushed and pushed, cursing the monster which now dominated their lives, forcing them to do this impossible thing under a cruel, merciless sun. Once Schirmer stumbled and lost his grip. A mad panic seized him. If he didn't catch the truck, they'd lose a metre or more! He grabbed for a stanchion. It ripped the length of his knuckles. He screamed with pain, but he held on.

Metre by metre they crawled up that terrible slope, fighting the monster ever upwards, each fresh step executed by naked will-power, *pushing, pushing, pushing,* fighting for breath, their lungs sounding like cracked ancient leathern bellows, as the air wheezed through them.

Once they came to a patch of soft sand and were reduced to sobbing, broken children, pushing the monster on their knees, millimetre by millimetre, eyes glazed, seeing only the next minute area of sand, before they managed to conquer it.

It was beginning to grow dark and Schirmer knew they

could go on no longer. 'Schulze,' he croaked in a broken voice, 'get ready . . . Gonna pull the brake.'

'Pull,' was all the exhausted giant could say by way of a reply.

Together they collapsed into the sand, gulping for air like stranded, dying fish, unable to see, speak, even think . . . and on the horizon the evening cooking fires of their pursuers burned unseen . . .

They started again well before dawn, their muscles stiff as boards, their tongues hanging out of their parched mouths like dry leather straps, hating the monster which had now taken possession of them and abused their poor, torn, exhausted bodies so mercilessly. Now they were getting ever closer to the top, but Schirmer, his body racked with pain, his muscles ablaze, dared not think of reaching the summit. That would be too great a luxury, for he knew that all his body demanded now was to be allowed to lie down in the sand – and die. No, they had to fight on. Another hour passed and they were only some ten metres from the top. '*Pause!*' he gasped and, pulling the brake, dropping sobbing for breath on to the sand, burying his head into his burning, blistered hands.

Schulze slumped where he stood, too weary to move into the shade, great chest heaving with that terrible effort, eyes glazed and dull, almost unable to take in those tiny black figures far, far away in the shimmering desert, pausing every now and again and gazing at the sand, as if they were trailing something. Slowly, very slowly, the realization dawned on him. '*Slopeheads*,' he said, '*spotted* trail . . . *following* us . . . Colonel,' he brought out the words in little gasps, like an idiot who found it difficult to put even the simplest of sentences together.

Schirmer did not react. He still slumped there, head in his hands.

'Damnit, sir!' Schulze called out with sudden exasperation, staggering to his feet blindly, 'they're out there . . . *They're after us . . . Come on!*'

Schirmer was roused by the urgency in the big NCO's voice. He, too, managed to rise again. He stumbled to his position at the wheel and pulled off the brake. Schulze bent his back once more to the rear. '*Los, mensch!*' he pushed. The torture commenced once again . . .

Metre by metre they crawled forward, groaning and moaning as the truck headed for that impossible summit. Now the Arabs were riding full out across the desert and, without looking round, Schulze knew from their faint, excited cries that they had been spotted. Digging his heels in, his muscles cracking and groaning under the hellish strain, he heaved and heaved.

They were almost there. Soon they would begin the descent. But would the monster start?

Schulze gave one last desperate shove. The truck tottered to the summit and balanced there, rocking slightly back and forth. Schulze flashed a glance behind him.

There were six of them racing all out, bent low over their mounts, their manes flying in the breeze, newly looted weapons balanced across the bony pieces of the horses' skulls, ready to fire when they were in range. Soon the leader would reach the bottom of the ascent.

'Get in, sir,' Schulze cried, 'get in for Chrissake!' He shoved hard and began freeing the automatic pistol he had taken from one of the dead Headhunters.

'Schulze—'

'*Nix Schulze!*' he cried angrily. 'Who's got the muscle in this outfit? Put her into second gear . . . come on, sir, at the double now!'

Schirmer protested no more. He swung himself inside the cab. With both hands, their cruelly lacerated palms running with blood, he thrust home the gear that had not been worked for so long. But it worked smoothly enough.

Schulze grunted. The leading tribesman was floundering up the ascent, his horse panting hard, slower now as it sank up to its fetlocks in soft sand. He heaved. The truck swayed back. Schulze exerted all his remaining strength, the purple vein ticking dangerously at his forehead, his eyes bulging.

Schirmer swallowed hard. The first slugs were already erupting in vicious little spurts of sand all around. It would not be long before they were overrun. The monster *had* to start! The truck tipped over the top and he hissed a fervent prayer. Slowly and ponderously it started to gather speed. From behind he heard a piteous scream of pain. He flashed a look in the rear mirror. A tribesman was rolling beneath his dying horse, scarlet blood spurting in a great glistening fountain from where its left eye had been.

'*Schulze*,' he screamed, '*get aboard!*'

'Not yet!' Now the big noncom was running behind the truck, as it gathered speed, hardly exerting any pressure. But the riders were gaining on them, too. In the mirror, he could see their brown wolfish faces underneath the flying head-dresses all too clearly. They were gaining on the ponderous truck rapidly.

Schirmer held his breath. This was it. He slammed home second gear. He hesitated for a fraction of a second. He let out the clutch. Violently the truck heaved. A black cloud of smoke erupted from its exhaust. It shuddered as if it might disintegrate at any moment. Schirmer thrust his body forward, willing the monster to start. Nothing happened. The motor did not start!

'Give it another chance!' Schulze yelled, hanging onto the tailboard with one hand. 'For God's sake!' Hardly taking aim, he fired. An Arab trying to outflank them so that he could get level with Schirmer in the cab flung up his hands and vaulted from his saddle. Next instant he went down under the flying hooves of those following.

Schirmer flashed a look ahead. The truck was gathering speed again, with Schulze running all-out. There was about twenty metres of descent left. After that came flat desert littered with boulders. If the damned monster didn't start by then, they would be finished!

Fifteen metres . . . ten . . . Schirmer knew he could wait no longer. Eyes frantic with worry, breath coming in great sobs, he let out the clutch.

Again, the truck shuddered violently. Behind him, Schulze held onto the tailboard for all he was worth, with the leading Arab only ten metres or so away, sword outstretched over the glistening neck of his mouth, swarthy face set in a grim smile of triumph – was coming in for the kill.

A long low moan. More shudders. A soft keening like some Breton piper's dirge. Thick black smoke was pouring from the exhaust. The noise grew in intensity. The truck shuddered at every plate. The Arab dug his spurs into his horse's flanks, aiming the blade directly at the centre of Schulze's big shoulders. It seemed as if the truck would blow up at any moment.

A series of sharp cracks. Here and there, a horse whinnied with terror. Still Schulze's pursuer kept on coming, bit held cruelly in place so that his horse could not shy. In a moment he would raise his sword and slice deep into the big man's shoulders. A burst of white smoke. Angry red and purple sparks followed from the exhaust. Abruptly there was the tremendous roar of the engine coming to life. Suddenly the truck was shooting forward and the Arabs were left behind, reining in their sweating horses, knowing already that their prey was going to escape – there was nothing they could do to stop them now.

Schirmer gunned the engine furiously while Schulze stumbled and sprawled full-length in the back, laughing crazily as he lay there, swatting at the slugs flying all around with his bleeding, blistered hand as if they were flies . . .

One day later the Piper Cub, sent by Colonel Mercier, found them. Twelve hours later, Colonel Erwin Schirmer thrust open the door of Colonel Comte de Gray's quarters, while Schulze covered the blue-clad *regibats* with his machine-pistol.

The tall aristocratic traitor was unexpectedly calm, as he faced the German with his white-bleached hair and eyebrows, his face hollowed out to a leathern skull by the suffering and privations he had suffered. 'I always knew it would end like this,' he said slowly, adjusting his elegant tunic and drawing himself up to his full height. 'Well, German?'

'Have you anything to say in your defence?' Schirmer rasped as, outside, the alarm bells sounded and police whistles shrilled – for the garrison had been alerted that the little plane had brought with it the German killers.

'Not much, German. You ruined us in 1916 at Verdun. We have never recovered. We French are a selfish people.' He shrugged eloquently, carelessly. 'I suppose I have been more selfish than most . . . All right, German, do what you have to do.' He gazed at Schirmer, no trace of fear on his handsome pervert's face.

Across the square under the shade cast by the palms, the blue-clad military gendarmes were forming up. Scared or not, they would charge in a moment. There was no time left. Schirmer's knuckles whitened as he began to squeeze the trigger.

Outside Schulze sang in a crazy drunken bass: *'There was once an old man of Rees . . . who swallowed a packet of seeds . . . Great tufts of grass . . . shot out of his ass . . . and his prick was covered in weeds . . .'*

'The supreme irony, German, you killed my father in 1918 and now in 1956 you . . .'

Schirmer fired. The pistol exploded in his hand. The noise was deafening in the tight confines of the shuttered office. The Frenchman slammed against the whitewashed wall, a great scarlet flower blossoming on his chest. Slowly, very slowly, he started to sink down the wall, trailing blood behind him. Schirmer dropped his pistol. He would never use a firearm again now. Head held erect, he walked out into the sunshine and what was to come . . . He had paid his final respects to his dead Headhunters.

ENVOI

'Gentlemen-rankers, out on a spree. Damned from here to Eternity. God have mercy on such as we. Baa. Yah. *Bah!*'

Kipling: *Gentlemen-Rankers*

They sat in the café in front of the *mairie*, facing the memorial to the 'glorious dead', sheltering under the French Marianne holding a furled *tricolore*. Around them, unshaven old men in grubby berets drank *rouge* with gnarled, work-worn fingers. The air was heavy with the scent of geraniums – and horseshit.

'You've grown fat,' Schirmer said and raised his glass of cognac in a toast to the one-armed ex-colonel.

Mercier smiled and raised his glass, 'And you, my dear Schirmer, have grown even thinner.'

'The diet at the *Cherche-Midi*[1] is not exactly the best,' Schirmer answered, watching Schulze as he emerged from the little town's sole brothel, doing up his flies and whistling happily to himself, 'the dirty water', as he called it, off his chest at long last.

'I worked as fast as I could to get you out,' Mercier replied, while Schirmer studied him, noting how old he seemed to have become, the eyes pink from too much drinking, a slight trembling nervousness of the fingers which hadn't been there before. 'But, of course, I was under suspicion myself. If I had not resigned, I suspect they would have risked a court martial in spite of the bad publicity.'

'I know, Mercier, I know,' Schirmer said hurriedly. 'You did your best, but after all, although de Gray was a traitor who had a good deal of blood on his hands, he was French and I . . .' he shrugged.

'A Boche,' Mercier completed the sentence for him. 'Of course, and we no longer have any need of you, do we? Our Empire has gone, those bastards in Paris have lined their pockets enough, done their deals with Moscow and the Slopeheads back in North Africa. What need is there now of Schirmer's Headhunters? If only we had disobeyed the Americans at Suez. One more week, *non*, a single day and we would have rubbed Nasser's long nose in his own

[1] A prison in Paris.

dirt and that would have been that.' He shrugged eloquently. 'Those damned, damned Americans' he cursed bitterly. 'What do they know . . . what indeed?'

Schirmer grinned at his red-faced indignation. Over the road, Schulze had opened the door of their little *deux chevaux*, which they had bought for their journey back to where it had all started. It sagged alarmingly under his weight.

'They pay better than the French, though,' Schirmer said softly.

The one-armed ex-Legion colonel flashed him a sharp look, as Schulze slammed home the awkward gears of the car, sending the chickens picking in the *pavé* squawking for cover. 'What is that supposed to mean?' he snapped.

Schirmer's grin broadened. It was nice to spring a surprise on Mercier, just this once 'What I say.'

'You mean the Americans have . . . approached you?' he asked, somewhat incredulously, as Schulze braked to an ear-splitting stop, flung open the door ceremoniously and then, for some reason known only to himself, took a large pair of red silk knickers from his pocket and hung them on the car's wireless aerial. He stood there beaming at the two ex-officers, while locals spilled even more *rouge* in their astonishment at the spectacle.

'Well, let us say, my dear Mercier, I am going back to where I started as a young cadet, still wet behind the spoons, in 1935.'

'1935 . . . young cadet,' he echoed, running the facts through his excellent memory. 'Why,' his eyes flashed alarmingly, 'in 1935, you were at the SS *Junkerschule*[1] at . . . Bad Toelz!'

'Exactly.'

'And Bad Toelz is now the home of the 10th US Special Forces Battalion!' he stuttered.

'The Green Berets, as they call them,' Schirmer said, enjoying his last triumph before they set off. 'A couple of thousand years ago, Mercier, the Roman Empire aban-

[1] SS cadet school.

doned the praetorian guards, so in the end they came back from Africa and started electing their own emperors. They say it was the end of the Roman Empire.' He shrugged carelessly. 'I don't know . . . and I don't care. All I know is that I am going home – courtesy of the US Army. For the time being, I can be a free man in my own homeland.' He rose to his feet and stretched out his hand. Awkwardly Colonel Mercier did the same, while the old men gawped open-mouthed. 'There will be a price to pay for it sooner or later, I know that. Mercenaries always pay in the end. But what matter? I'm going home.' He pressed Mercier's hand hard and the smaller Frenchman returned the pressure, sudden tears in his eyes.

'Don't think too harshly of me – or France, Schirmer,' he said, his voice thick with emotion. 'In 1945 when I forced you to join us from the prisoner-of-war camp I thought we French still had a chance. It was a gamble . . . it did not pay off. *Allah-i-chouf*, Schirmer!'[1]

'*Allah-i-chouf*, Mercier!' Schirmer echoed the old greeting and then he was striding imperiously towards a waiting Schulze, like a man who was in a great hurry.

Schirmer's Headhunters were going home . . .

---

[1] Literally, 'Allah sees us.'